I0690572

BOUNTY HUNTERS
AND KICK-ASS COPS

First Edition

Published by the Nazca Plains Corporation
Las Vegas, Nevada
2013

ISBN: 978-1-61098-352-5
E-Book: 978-1-61098-353-2

Published by
The Nazca Plains Corporation ®
Paradise Rd, Suite
Las Vegas, NV 89109

PUBLISHER'S NOTE
Bounty Hunters and Kick-Ass Cops is a work of fiction created
wholly by *Tim Brough's* imagination. All characters are fictional and
any resemblance to any persons living or deceased is purely by
accident. No portion of this book reflects any real person or events.

Cover, Thom Magister
Art Director, Blake Stephens

ACKNOWLEDGEMENTS

Hello Again, Gentle Reader.

Once upon a decade, you had to find an adult bookstore or some other store of similar repute to find anything like you've just purchased. Not that this was a bad or evil book, but there was a societal urge to make finding anything sexual – especially kinky – as difficult a task as possible.

The internet did a great deal to rid us of that problem, and now e-readers do us one better. No more secret stash under the bed or in the bottom drawer of a closet file cabinet. I hope someone, somewhere, is reading this on an airplane or bus, a park bench or beach lounger, where a book of such stories might have previously been a tad embarrassing for you or your neighbors. Electronic readers have found a need, and authors now get to fill it.

It's been some time since I compiled a batch of short stories. I've completed two works of non-fiction, *Skin Tight:*

A Guide to Rubbermen, *Macho Fetish and Fantasy* and *First Hand: An Erotic Guide to Fisting*. I've been working on these stories in various times, the earliest dates to 2001, the latest ("Bounty Hunters") December of 2012. You can get a lot done when you're not working at a job for a prolonged period.

So between playing with my beloved Sophie Cat (who has since gone to the rainbow bridge), helping Papa Joel around the house, and trying to come up with inspiration, these stories were crafted. I've been working on another piece of fiction that isn't dirty words oriented, and the biography of a kinky cop (which is my usual fare of BDSM goodness). Look for these in a coming year. It's a dirty job, as they say.

However, no author worth his salt can do this by himself, so hearty thanks to my Papa Joel, Thom Magister, Master Trooper, Master Malik, Herbert Moseley, Dr. Bob Rubel, Dave Rhodes, Dr. Larry, Alex Ironrod, GW Leatherman Parks, Peter Fiske, Joseph Bean, Paul Bright, Mark Weigle, all the guys of Delta and anyone else I may have left off.

Now turn that page and enjoy.

Tim Brough, Winter 2012

DEDICATION

To Alan Treiber and Dave Parkins, at <u>StationHouseVideos.</u> <u>com</u>, for handing me a DVD of "Kick-Ass Cops" a few years ago and suggesting I novelize it.

And probably never expected me to get it finished. Thanks for your patience, guys!

BOUNTY HUNTERS
AND KICK-ASS COPS

First Edition

Tim Brough

CONTENTS

FOREWORD

One of my professors once commented that, "All writing is fiction. Even so-called non-fiction is filtered and restructured by the mind of the writer." Everything we read is based on what was, what is, and what could be. A good story often combines all of these elements to draw us into an unfamiliar experience that will give us pleasure.

Fiction and fantasy have the ability to transport us into realms of the unknown. But this surface unreality must be grounded in some aspect of a deeper reality. Hamlet, in his speech to the actors, reminds them that the play holds a "mirror up to nature" and allows the audience to see the virtues and vices of the characters.

Fiction, like theater, holds a mirror up to nature and allows the reader to experience actions and ideas that may, at times, reflect a darkness not generally seen in reality. And, at times, these visions can awaken the reader to a new realty – a new yearning and desire.

These stories often illuminate that darker nature and are carefully crafted to explore and expose themes of betrayal and brutality. Blood is drawn, and – sometimes – the wound is kissed, and – other times – it is ignored or deepened. In the best circumstance, pain is a gift given generously. And, at times, it is selfish and gratuitous. Not all of the recipients are thankful or grateful. Not all of the sadists are lovers as well. These stories are often dark mirrors and not every reader will see their own reflection – yet.

And, these stories take us on a series of journeys – or explorations. One story travels through time, weaving together momentary fragments in order to reveal the final tapestry of pain and passion. Another explores the complexity, and morality, of artificial life in the form of androids.

Conversations, both internal and external, explore the desire for pain and the pleasure given and received by Master and slave. The age-old question of how this exchange transforms each partner begs the greater question of a kind of envy. At what point in the experience does the Master envy the slave? And vice-versa. Many have explored this mystery by changing roles. "Why am I here?" is often asked by both Master and slave.

These are thoughtful stories that are, it seems, intended to give the reader a "hard-on of the brain." They are not simply suck and fuck tales, but rather dark tales of torture, blood, and pain. They are both brutal and romantic. Not the romance of a Hallmark card but in the romantic gesture written in blood.

We are introduced to this collection of men without too much description of how they look. We are instantly transported into their minds and invited to explore their thoughts and actions as if they were our own. This is an opportunity to live, and experience, a different life. For some it will be new, and perhaps frightening, while others will find it familiar terrain.

If, what my professor said is true, then fact and fantasy are always conjoined. These stories may be fictional but there is a reality infused in them that will provoke a real response in the reader.

And if you find yourself in unfamiliar territory that makes your cock hard, so much the better.

Thom Magister
Author of *The Slave Journals*

IN MEMORIAM

To those men who inspired me, now gone:

Peter "Rubber Bear" Tolos
Mikal "Daddy Zeus" Bales
Paul "Papa Bear" Sehm
Ronnie "Bear" Borders
Dr. Phillip R. Reeves
Gary Gordon Taylor
Larry Townsend
Wayne Griffith
Ken Chomont
Roger Hickey
Rob Cole
And my dear, sweet Sophie Cat
I think of you all, every day, with deepest respect and love.

KICK-ASS COPS

Part 1: Capturing Brian

Brian's boots crunched the gravel. The sun was bearing down on the hot Georgia asphalt, and the fresh cuts in the side of the road just seemed to amplify the heat. He could feel the sweat trickling down the back of his t-shirt as the wavy heat mirages shimmered above the open paving. The walk home was going to be long. Brian didn't know which prospect he was dreading more: the three-mile walk home in this heat, or getting home and telling his older brother, Gunner, he had just blown another job interview. He heard another car approaching, so he turned around and stuck his thumb into the air.

The car just rolled past. "Dammit," Brian cursed under his breath. If he could get a ride, at least he'd get out of this heat, and he could get the aggravation of dealing with Gunner over with. He kept walking and his sweat kept pouring, minute by humid Georgia minute. The heat was really wearing him out when he heard the rumble of another motor coming up behind him. Brian turned to extend his thumb, and just as quickly pulled it back as he recognized the black-and-white. He cursed under his breath again as the police cruiser rolled past, the officer glaring through the window and his mirrored shades. Hitchhiking was still a misdemeanor offense in King County. A ticket was the last thing he needed for Gunner to hang over his head.

The cruiser pulled a little further up the road just far enough for Brian to get a sense that he may have dodged the bullet on this pass. But then he heard the grinding sound of tires making a U-turn and the pit of his stomach fell. He turned as the siren barked a warning and the cruiser came back up the road. The officer got out of the car and glared at Brian through the reflecting shades. "This isn't going to go good," he thought to himself.

The cop shouldered up to Brian and snarled, "Put your hands on the car." Confused, Brian protested and tried to turn on the charm. He didn't think he had done anything wrong, and tried to deflect the cop's seeming hostility. His nametag read Malloy, and he wasn't in a mood to be talked back to. He tucked his cigar in his jaw and pushed Brian into the hood of the car. "Spread those legs a little bit," he snapped as he roughly ran his gloves across Brian's sweaty shirt. "Keep your mouth shut and we'll get this squared away." Malloy began slapping and squeezing, feeling the kid's muscles, guessing how much they could take if he decided he wanted Brian for his special services.

When Brian's hands landed on the hood of the patrol car, the burning sensation made him jerk back. "I wasn't doing anything wrong! I was only hitchhiking," he objected, only to feel a gloved hand grab his crotch and give it an unsubtle squeeze. "Hey! Watch what you're touching there, bud!" Malloy blew a huge cloud of cigar smoke in Brian's face in response. "That cigar stinks!"

Malloy pushed his suspect down back against the hood. "You don't watch me," he sneered, "you watch that black hood." He continued to pat down Brian with increasing harshness, knowing he was pushing this punk towards making a mistake. He laid one more hard slap across the kid's crotch before he decided to give him a special ride. "You know hitchhiking's against the law." As soon as Brian started to resist, Malloy whipped out the cuffs. "Give me that left hand." He wrestled Brian's arm around his back and slammed the cuffs across his wrists.

Brian cried out in pain. "That hurts!"

"It's *supposed* to hurt," Malloy replied. When Brian tried again to argue, Malloy pulled Brian's sunglasses off his face and threw them on the hood of the cruiser. Squeezing Brian's face in the grip of his glove, he pulled his face tight against his. "When you talk to me, you take those sunglasses off. You understand me?" When Brian nodded, Malloy pushed him into the rear door of the cruiser. But instead of opening the door to get his prisoner into the back seat, he reached inside the front to pop the trunk. "We're going for a little ride."

"I don't think so!" Panic began to set in. Brian started to yell for help as Malloy lifted him up and tossed his cuffed prisoner into the trunk of the cruiser. "You're gonna pay for this," Brian yelled as he tried to kick the trunk lid from closing. "Fucking pig!"

"Keep your mouth shut for a while." Malloy jammed his fist into Brian's gut. "Don't let me hear that again." He slammed the trunk closed as Brian's muffled cries and obscenities became trapped within. He felt a rumble in his crotch as he stepped up to the front of his cruiser and grabbed the kid's sunglasses off the hood. "This kid needs a lesson," he thought as he revved the engine and took off with his passenger locked in the back.

Brian had no idea how long he was trapped in the trunk or how far they'd driven. He just knew it was dark and hotter than hell inside the back of the Officer's car. The cruiser even stopped a few times, but he never heard anyone outside, not even Malloy. He had already decided kicking the trunk was not a good idea, but he did try shouting a few times when the cruiser was parked in an attempt to get himself out of this mess. Dammit, he realized Gunner was probably wondering where the hell he was, and would kick his ass if he found out he'd been arrested. Even if the cop was a psycho. The car made an abrupt turn and a hard bump. There was some sort of reverberation in the engine sound and the cruiser went into park again. Was it a garage? Then the engine cut off as Brian heard the sound of a garage door closing.

Malloy reached under the dash and hit the automatic trunk latch. When he walked to the rear of the cruiser, he gazed down on Brian's sweat-soaked body and smirked. He looked to his right and saw the hood he'd left on a work chair just for his special guests. Wrapping his gloved hands tight around Brian's head, he squeezed his skull and ordered, "Come on up here." Jamming his handcuffed prisoner over the lip of the trunk, he reached over for the leather hood.

"This don't look like no fucking jail to me," Brian shouted as Malloy forced his diaphragm over the rear of the cruiser. The pressure on his gut made it hard to breathe, as Malloy pulled the multi-buckled hood over his head. "Fucking pig!" he gasped. "What the hell is this?" The leather scraped across his ears, pulling his hair.

"Stop asking so many questions," Malloy snapped, buckling the hood tight over his captive's face. Even with his lungs struggling to fill with oxygen, Brian was fighting the head sheathing. Malloy crooked his forearm around his prisoner's neck, scissored his muscle to hold him still, and secured the hood in place. Jerking his cuffed captive out of the cruiser, he hooked one arm across his neck and the other around his chest, even while Junior kept shouting and cursing. "Shut your fucking mouth!" he snarled.

Brian wasn't about to surrender easily – or silently. "You'll pay for this! Fucking pig!" He felt Malloy's massive chest driving him through a doorway, even as he tried to fight the inevitable force behind him. Malloy's arm was tight around his neck, with no way to stop the cop as he was muscled down a hallway. He felt a booted leg go ahead of his and he tumbled to the floor. The leather hood crushed into his face as Malloy threw his full uniformed weight across his back. The cuffs dug into his wrists with enough force to make him shout in pain.

There was a length of rope in the bedroom where Malloy had just driven his prisoner to the plush carpet. As Brian lay cuffed and face down, Malloy wrestled Brian's booted feet and crossed them over each other. Looping the rope over the boots till he'd drawn Brian's feet up tight, he roughly jerked Brian's wrists up and pulled the rope under the cuffs, drawing the rope tight and cinching Brian till he yelped, then pulling the rope back around the ankles. Brian struggled and grunted, but Malloy had him not only handcuffed but also hogtied and hooded. He slapped his gloved palm hard into Brian's hooded face and chuckled, "How do you like that?"

He stood over his helpless guest, swelling with the thrill of his catch. He turned to the wall of his bedroom, which he had lined with mirrors. The reflection from his wall multiplied into a strange funhouse infinity from the mirror shades he'd yet to take off. It was time for Malloy to begin his ritual.

Part 2: Malloy's Ritual

There were three people in the room now. Brian, who was hooded and hogtied on the floor; Officer Malloy, who was feeling full of piss and swagger having landed his prey; and the reflection in the mirror that was staring back at the physical Malloy. When he had a captive in his house, Malloy had a procedure he indulged in before the real fun began. He'd already put the kid in his place, the struggling and grunting fed into the power he now knew he had over the prisoner. "Yeah," he reminded himself softly. "I'm gonna teach this boy a lesson."

The millions of Malloys that cascaded back from the mirrored shades dropped back to two as Malloy deliberately took the helmet and sunglasses off, placing them on a towel by the sink. They eyed each other down, the hard ass standing on the floor in uniform and the larger-than-life reflection. The hands watched as the gloves were peeled back, allowing the biceps to admire themselves. Malloy ran his naked hands through the thickness of his black hair, making sure that it was all in its most effective place. The sidearm was next; double checking the safety in the mirror before laying it down with the helmet and glasses. His duty belt slid away from his waist and he took in a chest-expanding lungful of air as he let his mind tick through the little games he was going to play with his prisoner.

Almost on cue, Brian began to fight in earnest once again. The huffs and struggles behind him made Malloy curl a corner of his lip into a smirking grin. This punk would be visiting the basement soon enough, he thought. He let out that breath in a long whistle, one he knew Brian had to hear even through the hood. There was going to be plenty of pain to come, Malloy thought. *But not a damn minute earlier than I'm ready for.* The Cop in the mirror smirked back as the tie came away from the collar, and Malloy carefully undid the top buttons of his uniform. The zipper slid down his chest as both Officers watched their massive, muscular chests flex free of the form fit of the uniform shirt. Malloy was damn proud of the strength he'd instilled in himself and his body. His chest hair formed a ladder up his stomach, emphasizing each ripple of his abdomen.

'*That punk on the floor may be in good shape,*' Malloy thought as he stared down the Officer in the mirror, '*but I can whup each and every single shit that gets on my radar.*' He reached down to the mirror shine of his boots, gripping them tight as he pulled them off from his calves. He kept them as sparklingly dark as he could, because – he chuckled – you never know when you might have to land one up some punk's ass. The grunts and snorts from behind him made him smirk again... those cowboy boots that kid was wearing weren't nothing compared to his Dehners.

Malloy zipped the seams along the pant cuffs, freeing the uniform pants to drop away from his hard thighs. Then he stood by the mirror for one lingering look. The way the deepness of his tan against the tight white undershorts highlighted his ass made him swell with pride. He knew if his prisoner didn't have the hood barricading his eyes to already terrify him, the view of this muscled, tattooed ex-Marine Police Officer would have put the fear of the almighty right deep down into his soul.

But a god must be pure before he can exact his punishments. Malloy walked to where Brian lay twisting and writhing, trying to hunch himself to a point that his hands might reach his tied ankles. Brian would try to lift himself, bringing his body almost to his knees while using his hooded head as a pivot. Malloy stood over his prisoner, watching the young man get his fingers so close to the ropes at his ankles, only to collapse to the floor before starting again. The captive's breaths were short and sharp, punctuated with grunts and wheezing. The sweat was staining the shirt and Malloy could see the chafing where the cuffs were biting the skin. Red rings were forming along the kid's wrists, glistening and smelling of exertion and sweat. Malloy opened the plate glass door to a standing shower, just in front of where his prisoner struggled in vain.

He will be rank with fear-stink, Malloy thought, but I will be clean. He turned the spigots 'til the hot water began to steam out from the shower. Before he stepped into his cleansing hot water, he dropped to his knee and grabbed Brian by his hooded head. Brian emitted a squeal of surprise, enough for Malloy to feel a rumble in his shorts. Lifting the hood off the carpet until Brian was turned sideways, he gave one last thought to his captive before his washing would start. "You ready to get out of there?" he teased. "I told you about hitchhiking, didn't I? There's a lot of crazy sons of bitches out there." With a rough shove, he knocked Brian back to the carpet.

As he stood back up, Malloy peeled his underwear down his thick legs and crossed into the stinging water. Through the glass door, he stared down at the twisting and struggling prisoner on his bedroom floor. He took the soap down from the shelf and lathered himself up, letting the pressure from the shower rinse away the day's dirt. His sweat, a real man's sweat, cop sweat, going down the drain so he could be pure, strong, ready to be everything this law-breaking punk never would measure up to. That's why men like Malloy had to teach them lessons, why Malloy had to work so hard to be almost super-human strong. Weak men needed to learn, and he was the man who could show them the error of their ways.

Malloy's soapy hands rubbed over each part of his masculinity, leaving a sudded trail across the hard muscles of his legs, the cut of his chest and hips. His hands moved in a circle around his crotch, slicking his cock into a semi-erection. His thoughts drifted to exactly how the lesson would have to be administered to his new student. The soaped fingers began to roll his nipples, as he began to visualize this new prisoner, downstairs, wondering what the hell was coming next. That rumble in his balls he had felt a few minutes ago returned, and Malloy stopped himself. He turned away from the glass door, away from the vision of his frantic, frightened, and helpless victim. The hot shower lit into him until he got his impulses under control. Oh yes, he told himself. He is going to get that final lesson. Later. Later, he reminded himself. Take the long haul. The water was rinsing what was left of the soap off Malloy's body and down the drain, along with the heated thoughts of burying his cop dick in his prisoner's ass.

"Not until he learns his lesson," he muttered to himself as he stopped the water's flow. He looked to the sweating, cursing hooded man just a few feet away. The only thing separating Malloy from Brian, as far as he was concerned, was self-discipline. Just like the glass wall of the shower door he stood behind. Clear, strong, hard... but breakable. I have to be strong, Malloy thought as he willed his erection into retreat. I have to stay clean.

Part 3: Brian's Captivity

Brian could hear the water of Malloy's shower through the hood. He kept trying to hunch himself to where his hands could possibly undo the ropes around his feet; maybe he could somehow run? But the tightness of the hogtie made even that limited range of motion impossible. All he could do was grunt and gasp, trapped. All because he couldn't get a damn job, he thought, why couldn't he catch a goddamn break?

The shower stopped running and there was a muffled creak. Brian froze long enough to feel Malloy grab him by the cuffs and pull his hogtied arms into a painful angle above his back. Through the leather over his ears, he heard the Officer bark, "When I untie your feet, you better not kick. Or I'll break your fucking shoulders."

Brian hit the ground with a thud, knocking the wind out of his lungs. He felt the ropes coming away from his back, and his feet fell down to the floor. A muscled bicep hiked under his chin, lifting him to a standing position as he felt Malloy forcing him forward again. "I have to go back on patrol, so you need to go to the guest room."

Once again, Brian felt Malloy's broad chest driving him forward until he realized he was at the brink of a stairway. He locked his knees in fear that Malloy was going to throw him down the flight of steps; instead, the naked cop shoved his arm through Brian's crotch and hoisted him in the air. With his head bouncing off the walls of the stairwell, Brian was carried to the basement. Malloy dropped him to the floor again, but this time there was no carpeting to cushion the fall. He felt a sharp pain spike through where he struck his arm against what he realized must be concrete.

There was a clanking and grinding sound again, and Brian felt the hood being pulled upon. The sudden light blinded him as Malloy grabbed his wrists and started to unlock the handcuffs. Before his vision could adjust, Malloy slammed him chest first into the wall. Brian was so stunned that he was unable to resist Malloy shoving him headfirst into a small rectangular opening. He fought to scramble out, but Malloy pushed him back with the sole of his foot. He felt his t-shirt pull over his head in the fight but a steel grate ultimately closed in front of him, leaving him confined in a box-like pen.

Malloy squatted down in front of the bars to Brian's cell. His naked chest was still damp from the shower and the exertion of carrying Brian into the cellar. "What do you think of my guest room, boy?" he laughed.

Brian pulled back into the cell as far as he could, fearful of what Malloy might be thinking of doing to him. But all Malloy did was stare at him, as if daring him to try and rush the bars. Finally, he muttered to his prisoner "I need to get back on duty. You can yell as loud as you want, but nobody's going to hear you down here. You just sit tight and think about what we're going to do when I get back."

A wooden panel slid down over the opening and closed atop the cell door. A darkness even deeper than the trunk of the patrol car enveloped Brian, and there wasn't a sound to be heard. If Malloy had walked away, he couldn't tell. Was he really back out on the street in his cruiser? Would he be back? What if he brought some of his psycho cop buddies back with him? And what kind of maniac locked people in a secret compartment in their basement?

Brian kicked at the walls with all the strength he could in the cramped space, but the walls were solid. "Let me out, you fucking pig!" he shouted, the tight cell only amplified his screams to a painful level.

The cell, he realized, was soundproofed. No noise was going to get out, and even if it did, he was in the basement of a huge house! How the hell would anyone hear him? Brian began to kick the walls in a panic, his cowboy boots echoing inside the chamber, but the blows were incapable of weakening the walls of his confinement. He gasped for breath in the darkness hard and short. In his mind, he realized he had to regain control. He began counting backward in his mind, downwards from 100, "Ninety-nine, 98, 97, 96, 95, 94..." as he got his panic under control again. Time slowed back down. Brian curled himself into a corner and closed his eyes to the darkness. All he could do was wait.

However many hours passed, Brian had no way of knowing, but he was startled by a sudden break in the silence – a scratching, lifting sound from outside. He cowered back as far as he could, but when the wooden cover pulled away, he could see the dark blue of Malloy's uniform pants; the pistol holster hanging menacingly by his hip. Brian was terrified, but he still tried to sound like he wasn't, "It's about time you came and got me out of here, Motherfucker."

Malloy pulled the cuffs away from his belt and reached inside for Brian's wrists. Clamping the cuffs closed, Brian was roughly hauled out of the cell. Malloy jerked him to his feet, and Brian said, "I don't know what the fuck you think you're doing..." the words were cut short as Brian's arms were pulled up over his head, stretched to the point where he thought his shoulder might dislocate.

"I know exactly what I'm doing," Malloy menaced. Taking another set of cuffs from a chain in the ceiling, he secured Brian. His arms were so stretched that his chest arched out, and he could feel Malloy move behind him. Gloved hands clutched Brian's throat as Malloy hoisted him up, snarling, "Stand up straight!"

Brian could only hop for balance as Malloy jerked each leg up to pull his cowboy boots off, then came back behind him and brought his hands to Brian's belt. Even though it cut into his wrists to fight, Brian twisted and squirmed. He couldn't believe this crazy-ass cop was tearing his clothes off! Malloy stripped Brian's pants away and tossed them across the room, leaving Brian dangling from his wrists clad only in his undershorts and too frightened to even scream.

He was so scared in his current predicament that he would have bargained to be back in the secret wall compartment. His attention then focused on the room. There were all varieties of chains, cuffs, hoods, gas masks, and other leather instruments that he couldn't begin to guess the usage of, and he began his struggles once again. Whatever the hell this psycho had down here, it couldn't possibly be good. He also realized that, even though they were in the basement of a house, Malloy wore his mirror-shades and crash helmet like he was still on duty.

Brian almost fell to the floor when Malloy reached to unchain his wrists from the ceiling. But he clutched the cuffs still on Brian's wrists and pulled him around the corner from the wall-cell; Brian instantly tried to escape. In front of him was some sort of huge padded table surrounded by paddles, floggers, and whips. The tabletop was tilted slightly with a padded ring at the head of it. A crisscrossing canopy of heavy-duty chains webbed the top of the frame, and plastic tubes and electrical extensions were fastened to the four posts that supported the entire apparatus. Brian pulled away from it with all the strength he could.

Malloy, however, was far stronger and swung Brian onto the table like a bucket on a rope while Brian flailed his legs to try and kick Malloy away. His back hit the leather-covered table with a thud. Malloy just smiled wickedly, grabbed Brian's throat with one gloved fist, and pressed his other arm hard across his forehead. "You better give it up now," he sneered as Brian gasped for air.

Taking advantage of Brian's position, Malloy snapped up a leather plug gag, squeezed Brian's jaw 'til it forced open, and jammed the wide leather bulb into Brian's mouth. All Brian could do now was whimper, almost to the point of sobbing. He felt like his forehead would cave in like a piece of fruit from the force of Malloy's arm against him. His eyes closed against the pain.

That was enough time for Malloy to close his gloved grip around Brian's neck, and he snarled as he spun Brian around. Malloy picked him off the floor and threw him face first. "Get your face in that hole," he ordered.

Brian tried to kick his way off the pads, but Malloy again used his forearm to hold him down. The hole had a foam donut, covered with leather, and was just wide enough that Brian's face fit inside the circumference. A wide belt of leather pulled across the back of Brian's head, and he couldn't resist the downward force as Malloy tightened the strap and buckled it in place.

"You need to calm down," Malloy growled. "Why don't you relax a little bit?" He removed the handcuffs on Brian's wrists only to pull each one into leather cuffs fastened on opposite corners. Once he had Brian secured to the head of the table, Malloy moved to the back where Brian's kicking legs were still loose. He clamped one to the table, and he had to duck as

Brian tried to land a kick. Twisting Brian's leg at a painful angle, Malloy barked, "Get 'em down and keep 'em there!"

Brian squealed into the plug gag, but he stopped kicking. Malloy wrapped more leather cuffs around each of Brian's ankles, spread-eagling him.

Brian could feel his limbs being secured (as he fought off). But there was no way to escape the muscles on this psycho-cop; eventually, Brian could do little more than squirm against the leather. His face was pressed firmly down against the padded black leather ring by a strap. The gag was biting into the corners of his mouth, but he remembered Malloy saying no one could hear any screams down here. Why the hell did he have to gag him? What the fuck was he getting out of this? Then he felt the slickness of cool leather across his back, another strap. Brian moaned. What the fuck? He felt the air forced out of his lungs as Malloy jerked the belt sharply over his back and buckled it closed.

Another strap slid across his lower back, and Brian again felt the sharp tug as Malloy secured that one as well. Eventually, Brian felt more leather bindings over his thighs and calves, making any and all resistance futile. The straps were so tight that Brian could feel his own pulse; his heart was pounding, which practically made those restraints tourniquets. Brian tried to divert himself by counting the beats, trying to gauge his pulse, trying to calm his terror. *'He's gonna pay,'* he kept thinking. *'I'll make this bastard pay.'* He felt something graze his thigh, then brush against his ass. *'You're gonna pay for this…'* Then the first blow landed on his back.

Part 4: Malloy's Lessons

Malloy looked over to his captive, wriggling under the tight leather straps. He could hear Brian's whimpers and the beginnings of sobbing. Those noises reverberated to his crotch, almost like a good stroking with a greasy hand. He had brought plenty of punks to his work room for private lessons.

The first being a young drunk about four years ago who'd taken a swing at him in an alley behind a bar. The stupid shit landed his fist into Malloy's helmet, probably hurting his punk hand more than anything else. But it was significant enough a blow to piss Malloy off, so he threw the punk into the side of a metal dumpster so hard that the punk puked on himself and passed out.

He looked so pathetic that Malloy became even more enraged. Rather than slap him around 'til he came to, Malloy cuffed the asshole and dumped him in the backseat of the cruiser. "I'm gonna teach you a lesson," he mumbled to himself as the vomit-stained punk moaned in the back.

Malloy drove back to his home with the semi-coherent drunk. He parked his car in the garage then carried the kid downstairs to his tool bench. He took a few bunches of clothesline and a dirty towel to tie the punk down, and then sat nearby and waited. It took a half-hour or so 'til sobriety took hold, but when it did, Malloy could make out every curse word this punk called out from behind the towel-gag. He'd tied each wrist and ankle to the legs of the tool bench, restraining his captive in a clumsy spread-eagle. Even so, he wasn't going anywhere, and Malloy was getting tired of the shouting. He silently rose from his chair and pulled a long strip of duct tape away from a roll on the workbench, then forced the towel deeper into the prisoner's mouth. The tape wrapped over the towel and cut off almost any remaining sounds. The punk was reduced to little more than jerking against the ropes, gurgling grunts for protests.

"Didn't anyone ever tell you public intoxication is against the law?" Malloy chuckled. But now that he had him, he thought, what exactly was he going to do with him? He couldn't just let him go home. He couldn't just tell the punk that he was getting off with a warning. He scanned the scattered junk on the workbench 'til his eyes fell upon an old uniform belt he used to hold boards together with. Taking the belt off the bench, Malloy trailed it along the gagged cheeks of his prisoner. "I can do two things," he told the struggling youth. "I can either write you up for public drunkenness and assaulting an officer," he paused to snap the belt for effect, "or I can beat your ass 'til you tell me you're sorry and that you'll never take another swing at a cop."

The prisoner's screaming escalated; he was obviously ready to apologize. Malloy just laughed, "What makes you think that it was your choice?"

He moved to the back of the tool bench and used cop-muscle to jerk the pants away from his captive's rear end. "Time to teach you a lesson." The belt swung over Malloy's head as he brought it down with all the strength he could across the white undershorts. A high-pitched scream erupted from the gagged man's head while Malloy thrashed the man's ass over and over. He didn't remember how long he kept lashing that helpless ass, but he did remember when the young man burst into tears. Because as soon as the crying started, Malloy felt his erection explode into his uniform pants. He'd taught this punk a lesson... and he suddenly knew his role on the King County Police Force.

It hadn't been easy, but Malloy's workshop began to take on a more sinister shape. The Internet held a wealth of resources to flesh out the basement, and Malloy was crafty enough to design a lot of his own instruments. It was his idea to partition off part of the support wall for an isolation cell. He'd discovered a website that offered instructional guides for bondage racks and tables. He'd come across a barber's chair during a random search on E-Bay. As his ideas became more intricate and his encounters increasingly sadistic, Malloy also discovered an age-old BDSM axiom: all stores are toy stores. Sporting goods stores, medical equipment shops, even the classifieds held hidden treasures.

Once, Malloy placed an early bid on the contents of a storage unit that had been seized during a warranted search before the items were listed. It had been part of an investigation into a suspected narcotics and prostitution ring, but the raid on the unit yielded none of the expected substances. It turned out that while the perp was into prostitution, he was also into BDSM. The unit had been conveted into a makeshift torture chamber. Once he was taken into custody, several of his call girls testified that he had a few kinkier clients who would arrange to visit the storage unit for the more esoteric thrills. There were rows of floggers, cases of cuffs, and an array of bondage gear that would've made the Spanish Inquisition proud. A Dominatrix, who broke her silence on the investigation, indicated that some rather prominent figures would be embarrassed if this discovery were made public. Therefore, it was kept under wraps, and Malloy and his men waited the investigation out until the narcotics charges were bulletproof.

All that gear, because it was seized in the course of a drug investigation, suddenly became the property of King County. Malloy sensed his opportunity and put in a silent bid through a third party he had learned of during the investigation. The third party was one of the leading figures on the list of clients to frequent the storage unit, as was teh auctioneer. The night before the sale was to take place, "Lot 227-A: Contents of a Storage Unit seized in the course of Operation Kingdom Come" was listed as sold. It never even made it to the auction block. Before the auctioneer's gavel opened the sale the following morning, Malloy had already started hanging the floggers along the wall adjacent to the bondage frame he'd built just a few months before.

The same bondage frame on which he now tightened straps over Brian. The prisoner was twitching and squirming, but those straps made all these boys the same. The row of floggers drew his attention to the next step in today's lesson, and he ran the fingers of his glove through the tendrils of one fashioned from thick black leather. He lifted it from the wall and let the leather tongues slide through his thumb and forefinger. The corner of his lip curled as he looked at the ass on the table, clenching and twisting under the leather straps. He stood to the side of his bound student, letting the flogger's tails caress Brian's leg. Goose bumps lifted to the surface of the skin where the leather brushed it; *'Good,'* thought Malloy. *'He's anticipating it.'*

As the cool strands of the flogger breezed over Brian's ass, Malloy took in the sight of tight white cotton undershorts ruffling under the black cowhide. Tiny contortions coursed along Brian's limbs where Malloy teased the flesh. Running the tails of leather through his glove, he stepped back ever so slightly from the table and reared back and swung the flogger hard across Brian's back. Malloy's reward was a harsh scream left confined by the leather plug blocking Brian's mouth. The first twinge of satisfaction fired through Malloy's spine as he hauled back and landed another, welting the first bars of red. The air hissed with leather, raining blow after blow from the flogger. The tan his captive had built over the summer was turning into a burning glow from the repeated strikes.

'That tan line must mean there was some non-tanned flesh,' Malloy reasoned. There was a pair of safety scissors kept on the workbench for just such curiosities. Letting the cold blade taunt Brian's fleshy ass cheeks, Malloy tore into the cotton undershorts with an audible snip, knowing full well that his prisoner could hear his last threads of protection about to be torn away from his body. He would be exposed, open, vulnerable. More to the point, the captive would feel the humiliation of being stripped naked by a superior police officer. The under-exposed white skin on the prisoner's ass was an inviting target. Malloy's flogging continued with renewed vigor. Skin this white was not permitted. Its paleness, and certainly not while the back was bright red from the constant leather-tailed strikes.

Floggers, however, were only part of Malloy's arsenal. He'd spent cash and time getting his workroom wall filled with floggers, paddles, and other tools to deliver lessons to special prisoners. Putting the flogger back to its numbered hook on the tool wall, Malloy selected a hard leather paddle as his next instrument. This particular paddle was given additional rigidity by a metal bar that stiffened not only the handle, but the blade section of the paddle as well. When that thinly padded steel band landed on a man's ass, he knew there was more than cowhide making contact.

Malloy slid his gloved palm along the edge of the paddle blade. He'd found this one in an Atlanta bar one night when he'd gone in late. One of his informants had clued him in to the small store in the basement, and the young man who sold the paddle to him was embarrassingly fawning. "Yes, Sir," this and "Thank You, Sir," that. His eagerness irritated Malloy to the point where, once he'd bought the paddle, he made it a point to get the boy's name and the car he was driving. Ten days later, a "routine traffic stop" near the bar gave Malloy a guest for the evening. Malloy always found amusement in the fact that the same men who would be trying to get his undivided attention in some seedy bar were oblivious to whom he was once he put on a uniform and got out of a police cruiser.

The poor bastard was scared stupid when Malloy cuffed him and pushed him into the back seat. When he took a turn down the side of a hill along the outskirts of town and cuffed the clerk to a tree, the prisoner was begging Malloy not to hurt him.

"What did I ever do to you?" he wailed as Malloy pulled a strip of duct tape across the face of his captive. Just before tying a blindfold over the prisoner's eyes, he held up the recently purchased paddle and slapped it across his gloved palm.

"Don't you remember, boy?" Malloy smacked his palm again. "You took the cash out of my hand for this little baby." The eyes above the gag went wide with recognition as a terrycloth strip closed off the vision. But Malloy got that paddle to draw its first blood that night. When the blindfold got jerked free, Malloy could feel it soaked with tears. He left the salesman still gagged, cuffed to the tree by plastic ties. He gave himself one more spike of adrenaline by clicking a switchblade in the prisoner's face... and using it to weaken the cuffs. "They're compromised, boy," Malloy taunted the captive. "You work that little cut long enough, and they'll break apart. Then you can walk home. Maybe by morning – if you're lucky."

He thought about driving away from the patch of trees he'd left that punk in, how the darkness completely filled the space as his patrol car left him in the rearview mirror. Malloy's eye scanned Brian's newly bare ass as he weighed the paddle in his hand. Jostled it a bit, almost as if testing its weight before the first swing. The thinly sheathed metal bar hurt like hell, and Malloy felt his lip curl back when his captive jerked across the table and screamed into the gag. A bright white mark formed across the area of the blow, rapidly filling out with pink. That was just the first sting of color, Malloy knew. He was an artist. Colors were his forte. He would give this boy a lesson in appreciation.

Malloy's boots clicked the cement as he circled the table, intent upon his work. Crack after muscular crack was delivered across his captive's ass, until those pink welts began to deepen. Blooms of deep lavender rose as the blunt force continued, the white skin barely showing between the swelling high relief of the purple bruises. Sweat was darkening the blue on his uniform, filling his chest with a humid scent. Malloy paused to admire his work thus far, taking satisfaction in the groans still creeping out from the gag, even though the leather paddle's onslaught had temporarily stopped.

There was now a distinct crosscut of purple stripes, weaving across the prisoner's backside. The areas where the bruises and welts crossed the tan line formed a striking contrast: the bloody raised bars of the paddle's steel reinforcements, the bronzed skin exposed to the sun, and what little pale white border faded into the waistline. The prisoner was breathing hard, but steadily, his chest and shoulders shuddering with an occasional sob. Malloy knew that his work had fired off the captive's autonomic defenses, his pain receptors firing off frantic calls for adrenaline and dopamine. He could read bodies well enough to know that this one was probably "flying," trying to ride out the abuse being heaped upon it. Malloy also knew that, at this point, continuing to beat the prisoner at this level of severity might throw its body's inner circuit breaker and cause the punk to pass out from the pain.

The thought caused his lip to curl back. He hung the paddle back up and reached for the heaviest flogger on the wall. Bending body over the prostrate form of his victim, he whispered a promise into his ear.

"Remember punk, what I told you about hitchhiking? There's a lot of crazy people out there," he snarled, jerking the boy's hair in his gloved hand and pulling his head to one side. "They'd pick you up and kill you. I'd just like to hurt you." He hauled back on the flogger and let the blows rain hard and fast. The screams became long and drawn, but lower in their register. The body still thrashed, but the fight was weakening. Blood was pumping into Malloy's cock as he felt a spasm of precum dribble free from a raging erection. His mind raced with the thoughts about what he could do with an unconscious, bound ass. Yeah, Malloy thought, his uniform crotch filling out as he gave himself a sidelong glance in the workspace's mirror. His uniform was shining from the exertion of sweat and muscle. His mirrored shades stared back at him. A tight, bruised prisoner was losing this battle of wills. *'Yeah. I can make this one go nighty-night,'* he thought.

Part 5: Brian's Circuit Breaker

When that first flogger strike crashed into Brian's back, it took him completely by surprise. Even with this crazy cop tying him to this table in a room full of god-knows-what hanging off the wall, Brian still hadn't made the mental leap that his dangerous position would include getting his ass beat. The blows came down, harder and harder, stinging and pounding all over his body. It didn't matter how hard he tried to twist or turn, or how hard he tried to tighten his muscles in defense, there was no way to escape the torrent of leather that crashed across his back, shoulders, ass, and legs.

Brian kept trying to will the beating to stop. He tried to force the pain out of his mind, to will the panic down. He was getting pulverized by a King County Police Officer! Who would ever believe him? How would he ever get out of this? What could he do to make it stop? When he suddenly realized that the flogging had, indeed, stopped. He gasped for air, sucking down lung-fulls of oxygen around the gag that clogged his mouth. He tried to listen, but all he could hear was the click of boots across cement. His head was too tightly strapped down for him to try and get a look, but he could feel that nut-job of a cop nearby.

There was a sudden touch and tug at his hips, and he felt the waistband of his undershorts pull away from his body. A humiliated moan seeped from his mouth; Christ, was this maniac going to rape him after beating the shit out of him? A bolt of fear surged through his body when Brian felt cold metal tingle along his ass-cheek, then a short snip as the elastic got cut in half. Brian felt the sharp jerk of torn cotton abrasively coming off his body. The absence of even this small fragment of clothes made Brian feel all the more horrified. There was nothing between him and whatever this madman had planned. The void of action made him all the more terrified. What the hell was he doing?

It may have only been a minute or two, but it felt like purgatory in Brian's mind. It only mattered until something new crashed into his ass, a pain far more brutal than the leather strands of the first flogger. It was thick and solid; it felt like a crowbar was slamming into him. And this time, the cop wasn't beating him up and down his entire body. Whatever this sadistic bastard was hitting him with now, he was just using it to tear into his ass. Brian even recognized a pattern was forming. The hits were coming in a rhythm, and Brian also realized that the pain was coming in waves. Between screaming into the leather plug in his mouth and clenching his ass-cheeks in defense, each slam into his flesh lit up inside his brain. It was almost like Brian could see a basket-weave lighting up around the inside of his skull as the torturous beating went on and on.

Then something weird happened. Something Brian couldn't explain or understand, but suddenly a wave of sensations began to course through his limbs. His body suddenly relaxed in its bonds, like he had just fallen into a fast racing river and he was floating face down in the current. He could hear himself still screaming and heat was boiling through his ass and loins, but it was no longer the terrified torments that, just moments ago, had him in a panic. The crisscrossing fireworks in his skull muted out into a bizarre and comfortable white, with fused flare-outs pulsing into view when new blows were delivered.

The Cop must have noticed, because the beating paused again. Brian tried to get his breath, but this time the air only felt like he was filling his lungs with warm water. He knew he was still in deep danger, but there was some sort of euphoria throbbing in his mind. It was suddenly shattered when a hand pulled his hair and twisted his head over the table. Brian heard the Cop speak for the first time since the beating had started.

Brian heard him sneer, "I'd just like to hurt you." Brian felt a jolt of panic and fight race through his body again. He tried to scream, but as he did, the Cop began hitting him again. This time, it was like getting hit with a hard, heavy bag of belts, and Brian could feel the blows cascading all over his body like the earlier torture. He tried to fight it, but his strength was sapped. He attempted to will himself into taking it, but the white pulses in his mind raced back. Brian could still feel the leather crashing into his back and ass, but now each blow seemed like it was coming from far, far away. He felt like he was swimming underwater. Under very, very warm water. He thought he saw hands reaching across the end of the table for his, as he took flight off the table and into the Georgia sky. The throbs inside his mind, he thought, may not have stopped, but it didn't matter any longer. Was that his brother, Luke?

Something tripped inside Brian's head. Then he didn't think anything.

The beatings stopped, Brian thought. He felt the woozy fog of sleep trying to peel back from his mind, only to realize that the intense pain all over his ass and back confirmed what he'd thought he'd been through. But then he realized he wasn't on a table. The straps were gone, only a set of handcuffs restrained him now. For some reason, he had undershorts again…and the leather table was no longer supporting him. Brian was now crumpled across a plush, tan carpet and still in the house of that crazy-ass cop.

Part 6: *Malloy's Prisoner Gets Loose*

There was a moaning from off the side of the bed, where Malloy had turned his gaze. The prisoner was starting to come back to life after last night's introductory beatings. The hollow moans coming up from the floor made Malloy's lips curl back into a smile. He'd already gotten his pants and boots on, as he had to do a patrol today. But he'd already given thought to how the afternoon was going to go. He had every intention to give this punk some cop dick.

First thing though, was making certain this punk didn't get out of the house. He'd already cuffed him and pulled a pair of shorts on him – couldn't have him shitting the carpet – and his tight muscled body was rocking back and forth on the floor as he was rising back up from his rest. Malloy slapped him across the back and barked, "Wake it up a little bit." The captive mumbled and cursed, Malloy pushed him along the floor. There was a special item in his arsenal for this little punk, he reminded himself. Forcing his prisoner aside, he unrolled an Evac-u-splint across the carpet. Smoothing it out until it lay flat alongside the captive; Malloy grabbed the punk's ankles and jerked him roughly onto the blue plastic.

The prisoner yelped in pain as Malloy dragged his body into place. "What are you doing now?" he cried out. Malloy just pressed his flat palm into the kid's face, twisting his head sideways across the plastic, and commanded his captive to keep his mouth shut. Woven black straps crisscrossed the splint and Malloy began arranging them to bind the prisoner. Once the first straps were secured, Malloy unkeyed the handcuffs, eliciting another howl of pain from the punk as his arms bent into an awkward angle.

As each plastic safety buckle clicked into place, Malloy could feel the prisoner's will seeping out. He planted his boots on either side of the stretcher, knocking the captive's legs back into the center of the plastic. A smidgen of resistance was offered in the form of a feeble kick, which Malloy beat back with a fist to the calf. "Get your legs in there and keep them there," he snapped. When the prisoner muttered once more how he was gonna pay for this, Malloy just smirked and gave the webbing an extra hard pull.

Malloy kept cinching up the straps until his bare chest hovered over the captive's face. Roughly positioning the inflatable neck brace around the punk's neck, he finalized the strapping over the head area of the splint. There was another sharp yelp from the captive, and then a panicky gasping as he realized the straps and the neck brace were effectively choking off his air supply. Malloy stood back and watched for just a moment, relishing the fear he'd bundled up inside a piece of rescue equipment. Prolonging the moment just enough to make his own dick twitch; he let the webbing slip barely a notch over. It was just enough to free the prisoner's air passages, and once again make him blurt a declaration of revenge to come.

A swift boot-kick into the side of the plastic brought that to a halt, and Malloy snickered "How's that feel?" He even snorted out a laugh when the punk whined, "It hurts!" Drawing an air pump from along the wall, Malloy got back to his knees along the head of the splint. Lowering his face into his prisoner's he chuckled "You ain't felt nothing yet."

Malloy picked up the air pump, clipped the valve over the extension at the head of the splint, and began hand-pumping air into the plastic cells. The blue plastic expanded down the length of his prisoner's body, tightening around its limbs. The air lifted the entire contraption off the ground, levitating the body inside it and slackening the straps. Setting the pump down briefly, Malloy adjusted the folds of the plastic and tightened the webbing across the prisoner's chest. Picking up the splint by its carry handles, Malloy roughly shook the package to make the body inside settle into position.

The splint hit the carpet with a thud, and the prisoner bounced with a grunt. Resuming the pump action, Malloy steadily pushed the handle in and out of the metal tube. The hiss of forced air made the prisoner visibly cringe, with the expanding bladders tightening around the splint's frame. Malloy's boots were planted on either side of the prisoner's head, knowing full well that he was forcibly looking directly into his crotch and up upon his bare chest. He exaggerated the pump action a few times, making sure that his biceps and chest muscles flexed with menace. When the captive groaned again, Malloy paused. "That's not quite tight enough," he sneered. "We need a little more."

He set the pump just to the side of the prisoner's head and rapidly fired off a series of injections. When he felt physical resistance to his movements, he paused and taunted his prisoner, growling, "How does it feel around that head of yours?" He was met again with another lame threat of retribution, eliciting a bark of laughter. Pressing a few more pumps of air into the valve, he chuckled "Yeah, it's not tight enough." With a few more thrusts of air, Malloy was satisfied the splint would do just as it was advertised to do, and the prisoner would have no movement in his limbs that would cause increased damage or injury, should they actually be broken. He tossed the pump aside, allowing the thought of maybe breaking the punk's forearm later if he got too mouthy.

"I gotta go out and work today," he remarked casually, watching his prisoner rock back and forth in the tightness of the splint. The plastic rustled and squeaked with the struggle, making Malloy smile. "You just stay there 'til I get home." From inside the plastic cocoon came one snort of protest.

"Fucking pig."

Malloy spun hard, grabbed the splint by the carry handles near the head, and lifted it off the floor. The sweat he'd worked up from inflating the splint dripped from his chest, spattering the grey plastic around his prisoner's head. Dropping his voice to the register he knew could scare even the biggest badasses, he gave the body imprisoned within the splint something to mull over. "When I get home, boy, last night is going to feel like a day at the pool. And when I'm done beating you till you scream for mercy, I'm going to stick one big cop dick up your ass." He shook the plastic cage like a bag of rags and threw it back to the floor. "Understand?"

This time there was no snotty comeback. "I'll be back in a little while. Don't go nowhere." Yeah, Malloy thought, let him wonder what cop-rape feels like. He grabbed the uniform shirt from the back of his chair and headed for the garage, leaving the captive to ponder its fate.

Brian heard the door slam. He was scared that the bastard was setting him up, and that he'd burst back in any second to start pounding him again. His ass and muscles ached from the beatings, and having compressed air crushing into his calves made them come painfully close to cramping. The parting promise made him all the more freaked out; after everything he went through last night, the goddamn asshole was going to fuck him? He knew that if he didn't get free and get away, he might not live through the next assaults.

There had to be a way of getting loose from this damn thing, he thought. He started flexing his arms and legs, searching for any sort of give along the inner walls of his inflated prison. The brace around his neck offered no slack whatsoever, and pumping his legs left little room for motion. But the right arm found some sort of seam along which Brian could slide his forearm back and forth. He forced himself to concentrate on just that tiny crevice of space, working his arm along it over and over. Suddenly, he felt just a fraction more give along his arm, the sweat having made the inside of his encasement slick enough to try pushing his way up and out of the splint's side. He gave one hard thrust up, and there was a rush of coolness around his hand.

He'd done it…he'd gotten his right arm to a point outside this trap. With the sudden addition of free space, Brian started wiggling his left arm alongside of his body. He rocked and flexed until he gradually brought it above the lip of the splint, where he reached over with his freed right hand and pulled the opposite limb away from the inflated rim. The webbing bridging the top of the splint was now in his fingers, but the neck brace still held his head to where he couldn't see what he was clutching at. His frantic grabs raced up and down the straps, and his panicked thrashing had also managed to give his legs room to maneuver. The straps were no longer tight across his body, and Brian found his hands on one of the plastic clasps. He pressed and squeezed, twisting his fingers in every way he could bend them, until the heard the gratifying click. His arms broke free and the straps across his chest went slack. Brian was soon kicking his legs loose from the webbings, sliding his waist and twisting his back until he'd slid out from the bulk of the inflated chambers. Once he'd accomplished that, he had to twist and rock until slack along the plastic bladders absorbed the air from the neck collar, and a final grunting jerk freed his head from his restraints.

He'd escaped... or had he? Brian was still uncertain as to whether or not that insane cop had really left. Listening as hard as he could, Brian grabbed his crumpled pile of clothes from the corner of the bedroom and tread silently towards the master doorway. No sounds so far, so he gingerly opened the door and peeked out. He half expected a nightstick to come crashing down on his neck, but the house was silent. "Oh shit," he muttered, and dropped to the floor. As fast as he could, Brian pulled his pants and t-shirt on and spotted his boots still left in the hallway. Pulling them on even as he stumbled down the hall towards a doorway, Brian fled the room where he'd left the sagging airbag that bound him.

For a moment, Brian hesitated with his hand on the doorknob. The threat of another trap filled his mind, making his hand freeze. But the threat of "one big cop dick up your ass" echoed through his skull and he jerked the door open. He leapt through and barreled down a small set of stairs, only to realize he was in the garage where the cop had first yanked him out of the trunk and forced that leather hood over his head. Panic paralyzed him again, as – door... *'Door. Where is the fucking door?'* raced in his head. Sunlight dimly illuminated the slits in a Venetian blind across the room, and Brian bolted towards it. Pausing only long enough to ascertain that the coast was clear, he escaped the house and charged into a thicket of trees behind.

The sound of cars on a road was yards away, and Brian hoped that he might flag one down for help. His arms flailing in the air, the first vehicle to come by was a huge black SUV. It barely missed stopping in time, with Brian's hands slamming down on the hood to try and make the vehicle stop. But the driver only laid down on the horn and gave Brian the finger, squealing the tires as he sped away. The sudden, frightening thought that the next car just might be that crazy-ass cop drove Brian to run into the opposite field, vaulting a fence, and hoping that whatever the next road was he came across, it would be familiar enough to point him towards home.

Part 7: Brian Gets Home

The kitchen smelled of sweat and competition. Luke had managed to get a leave from the base, planned a surprise visit to his Mom and Dad, and his punk brother Brian. So far, he'd only rung up his Special Forces buddy Frank, who'd challenged him to a regular on-leave arm-wrestling match. Frank was Special Ops and worked out obsessively, so Luke rarely won. But this time, after a year of steady service, Luke had built himself up to the point where he was gladly giving Frank a run for his title.

Man-sized grunts were filling the kitchen as Frank tried to maneuver his elbow to a position that granted him greater leverage. He was surprised that Luke was actually strong enough to make this a real battle. Usually, a few seconds of pressure was enough to overwhelm Luke's arm, he'd slam his opponent down and claim another conquest over the US Marines. Not this time. Frank's forehead creased with exertion, as he growled with a last massive exaltation. That was what it took to make this challenge end just like the last three years' worth, with Luke's hand slamming to the table in defeat.

Luke stuck out his hand in a conciliatory gesture, huffing in air as Frank shook it. "I guess you did it again," he said, letting Frank savor his win. He stood up to get his dress shirt on…he wouldn't arm wrestle in it. Last thing he needed was an underarm sweat stain to screw up inspection when he went back to base.

Frank massaged his arm. This time was close, but he wasn't about to let on to Luke just how much he had to work for this win. "Get your shirt on, man. You look good. You do the uniform proud." Of course, he wasn't going to let him go without one last set of digs. "Y'know, no matter how much you bitch about how good you are, you're pretty strong. You've gotten pretty good, man! You're getting better, but never better enough."

"Of course, I'm still looking better than you," Luke retorted, adjusting his collar.

There was a uniform tie on the table that Frank picked up and let run through his fingers. "Seeing as we had to take all that land before you could get anything, you know we don't really worry about good looks. But you don't need to be the prettiest individual for being in, y'know, the Navy Seals." He leaned in to Luke and dangled the tie in front of him, mock sneering, "Jarhead."

Snatching the tie away from Frank, Luke chuckled. His old friend had been in the service as long as he had, even if they'd chosen different recruiting offices to walk in after graduation. They'd stayed close, shared stories and leaned on each other through two tours of duty, and shared a brotherly bond even when they were continents apart. Frank smiled back at him. They were family, even if not by blood, and they relished that.

"Mom and Dad will be glad to see you're home," Frank proclaimed. "Me, I'm glad you're back. Everything's gonna be all right, man. I missed you, really did." He watched as Luke fumbled with the necktie, and made room for one more jab. "We didn't have to wear these wimpy ties when we were in the Seals, y'know." He paused for a moment; then both laughed again. Frank gave Luke a fraternal punch in the chest as they heard the kitchen door open.

Brian entered the room, looking haggard and defeated. The low-sitting branches of the trees had caught his t-shirt as he'd run through the woods, tearing a gash in the chest from the collar to just above the belt line. There were cuts that tricked tiny beads of blood, and his face was smeared with dirt from where he'd fallen while trying to make his way back. He looked like someone who'd just gotten their ass-kicked.

Luke looked at his little brother and felt the contempt rising in his throat. "Where the fuck have you been?" he snapped. "Mom and Dad's been worried sick about you."

There was genuine surprise on Brian's face. "Luke, I didn't even know you would be here." He held on to the kitchen counter, trying to get his bearings after having run almost non-stop since escaping his captor. Limping over to the table that had just been host to the arm-wrestling bout, Brian planted his hands and sighed. "You wouldn't believe what fucking happened to me."

Pointing his finger at the chair Frank had just been sitting in, "Why don't you sit down in that chair and tell me," Luke ordered Brian. "Looks to me like you got your ass whupped."

Brian rocked himself in the chair. He was barely able to make eye contact with Luke. His eyes flicked back and forth between Luke and his buddy. Frank was a guy he'd never really liked. He knew Luke didn't think much of him, either, which meant that whatever Frank knew about him, it all came filtered through Luke's disgust. "Man," he finally said to Luke, "I gotta talk to you."

Raising his glass of iced tea for a swallow, Frank snarled. "So this is your piece of shit brother?"

"That's him," Luke nodded in response.

Ignoring Frank for the moment, Brian pressed on. "You may want to sit down for this. I was trying to come back from a job interview. I was hitchhiking when this fucking cop picked me up. But instead of taking me to jail, he took me back to his house, brought me down into his basement, tied me up, and started whipping my ass!"

His voice dripping with sarcasm, Frank stared Brian in the face. "If your Dad had whipped your ass a long time ago, you wouldn't have turned out to be the punk you are now."

Exasperated that Luke wouldn't even take his assault seriously, Brian slammed his palms on the table. Leaning forward intently, he yelled at his brother, "Luke! This cop! He can't just take you into his house, tie you up, and whip your ass! That shit's gotta be illegal!" He looked back towards Frank again, who was glaring at him with his massive arms folded across his chest. "Would you get this musclehead out of here?" Brian blurted.

After a moment, Luke nodded to Frank. "Alright Frank. Meet me by the pool."

Being told he needed to get out of the room by some punk, even his best friend's punk brother, did not suit Frank well. He snatched Brian by the throat and hoisted him up from the chair. Squeezing his cheekbones till his mouth pressed into a fishlike "o," Frank growled into Brian's face. "If you were my fucking brother, I'd be the one to beat your ass, you little fucker." He dropped Brian back to the chair hard enough to make it bend, and then stalked off to the patio.

His hands clutching his throat, Brian gasped "Luke, what's up with that guy?"

Luke's gaze followed his friend out the door. "Don't worry about him. He gets a little hopped up sometimes." He waited for the patio door to slam shut, and then turned back to Brian. "By the way, why did you want him to leave the room?"

Brian knew that just getting beat up by some nut-job cop wasn't going to score Luke's attention. Besides, Luke had beaten his little brother up more than a few times when they were growing up, so someone else wailing on him was probably justified in his mind. If he was going to make Luke listen, he had to take it farther. "I didn't want to say anything in front of your buddy," Brian lied. "But he fucked me." Well, he thought, he threatened to. That should at least be good enough. Brian also felt he'd judged correctly, since the claim had not been immediately bitch-slapped away.

His eyes grew dark as he stared back at his little brother. His little brother, with his shirt in shreds and his body cut and bloodied. "He done what?" Luke finally managed to exclaim.

"He tied me up and left the room," Brian extrapolated. "Then he came back and he fucked me."

Luke's fist balled up under his chin. His shoulders began to rock as his anger built. "A cop... took my brother... to his house... tied him up... and fucked him." He paused, staring at Brian for any hint that the story was bullshit. "A cop." Luke stalled, thinking. "I'm trying to get my head around this," he said softly. He may be a punk, he thought to himself, but he's my punk brother. He made another effort to absorb what Brian had just told him. "A cop took my brother to his house, tied him up..." his fist came back up to his chin as he struggled with the final revelation, "...and fucked him."

For one of the first times that he could remember, Brian saw his brother actually expressing something directed at him that wasn't loathing or disgust. Luke was going to believe the fake rape, and might even be willing to get revenge for his kin. Blood might actually be thicker after all, Brian thought. Would he be willing to retaliate? Pausing a few moments more, Brian offered one more crumb of bait. "I think we can find his house."

There was silence as Luke rested his chin atop his clenched hand. His eyes slowly lifted till they were locked with Brian's. "I tell you what," he finally said. "Why don't you get upstairs and get yourself cleaned up before Mom and Dad get home. I'll give this a little thought. Think you can do that?"

Brian didn't even say a word, but got up and left the kitchen. He'd told that crazy bastard he would make him pay for what he'd done, and he'd told a big enough whopper to get Luke into exacting retribution. He knew if he said much more, Luke might just catch on. As he left the kitchen, he grinned to himself as he heard Luke still muttering "A cop... tied him up... fucked him...a cop..."

From the patio, Frank heard Brian leave the kitchen and he went back to see what was going on. When he got a look at Luke, he knew that, whatever it was, it wasn't good. He hadn't seen his buddy this angry since he'd been turned down for a Marine scholarship. He'd slammed his fist into his truck windshield that day, and it'd taken 21 stitches to close the gash on his arm. To this day, they still joked about his 21-stitch salute. He tapped him on the shoulder, "Was'up, bro?" Assessing the look on Luke's face, he knew where this was likely headed. "What's a hot shit marine gonna do to the guy who beat up his brother?"

Luke knew that Frank would understand; this was family. Dishonoring one meant dishonoring all, and that just could not stand. "You're not gonna believe this, man." He leaned across the table to address Frank more directly, and then continued.

"He told me a cop took him to his house, took him down into his basement, tied him up, and fucked him."

"Took him and fucked him?" Frank asked, incredulous.

"Fucked him." The two warriors stared at each other, knowing what had to be done. "Tell you what. You want to have some fun? I want to kill this motherfucker."

Frank bolted up from his chair. His adrenaline had already kicked in. "Let's do it."

The two men pushed away from the table and went to tell Brian.

Part 8: Night Raid

Luke adjusted his night goggles by the car and gave Brian a silent signal to wait. They were lucky in that the moon was full, and little help other than a small flashlight would be required. The house was just off a small residential street, and the small thatch of trees behind it would give Luke and Frank enough cover to approach the house undetected. There was maybe 20 feet between the trees and the back of the house. Frank took the lead, waving Luke up to the sidewall, with little sound other than dirt under their boots.

The flashlight cast a shadow along the windowsill, and Frank gave it a test. It gave easily, and Frank snorted. "The stupid fucker left his window open," he lowly said to Luke. The men climbed in the kitchen, then followed the wooden floorboards. Brian had told them that a master bedroom was at the top of a flight of stairs, and the flashlights scanned the floor till the first step came into view. Luke flicked the beam as a signal to Frank, who started ascending the stairs. According to Brian, a double door at the top was the entry to the bedroom, and that was where they'd find the cop.

The floor creaked ominously under the two men's boots, but they saw the doorway exactly as Brian described it. Luke felt a surge of amazement; for a change, Brian wasn't making this shit up to get out of trouble. He pressed a gloved hand on the latch and pressed down; the door swung easily on its hinges. They could see a large man spread out across a king-sized four-post bed, snoring soundly. Keeping the light aimed low, each man went along a different side of the mattress. The massive shoulders moved up and down with each breath. Dammit, Luke thought to himself, this fucker's huge! No wonder he beat the shit outta Brian!

Just then, something set off the cop, and his arm flashed towards a pillow. Frank instinctively lunged at the hand, catching it just as it went for a hidden weapon. Frank squeezed the thumb joint until the cop's hand lost its grip, and then threw the gun aside. He put full pressure with his elbow into the cop's shoulders, forcing him down into the mattress. What he found odd was that the cop said nothing, other than to grunt and struggle.

There was a crack of handcuffs as Luke slammed them across the cop's wrists. Frank pressed his weapon into the back of the cop's skull. Luke ripped the blankets and bed sheets from off the cop and threw them to the floor, and grabbed the cop's underwear by the elastic band. "So you FUCKED my little brother?" With a great physical pull, Frank ripped the underwear in half and threw the pair to the side with the blankets. Undoing his belt and zipper, Frank snarled at his captive "I'm going to show you what it's like to really be fucked."

By now, Malloy knew he was in trouble. Serious, dangerous, trouble. He could feel the steel against his neck, and the weight of the muscular man pressing between his thighs. His mind began to quickly play through the scenario. With his hands cuffed behind his back to the point of them going numb, he knew there was no possible way to fight this off. And he did not question the fact that he was about to get raped. He'd already figured out that this was over the punk and he'd beaten on the night before. He'd been fucked before, but never by force.

As strange as it was, Malloy began to compartmentalize the event. This was going to be an angry fuck, and as such would be over quickly. He felt the spit of the man on top of him hitting his ass crack. It would only be seconds before penetration. Breathe, breathe, breathe. Maybe even less than 60 seconds. Again, he reminded himself, breathe, breathe, breathe. Malloy felt the pucker of his asshole go wide as his aggressor's cock split him apart. Mentally he counted, one thousand one, one thousand two, trying to pace himself against the violation. He could hear the snarls, the alpha animal grunts behind him, the cutting of the handcuffs into the small of his back. '*One thousand twelve, one thousand thirteen,*' he mentally clicked off.

There was no measure in this fuck, just a primal establishment of order. He'd broken the rules and the man on top of him was there to set the record straight. '*One thousand twenty seven, one thousand twenty eight;*' the pounding increased in frequency, the grunts in their pace. This may be a revenge fuck, but one thing Malloy knew, this would not stand. If there was revenge to be had, ultimately, it would be his. Suddenly, an explosive grunt burst from behind him, and Malloy felt the pulsing in his ass.

Mentally he sneered. Less than 30 seconds, that was all he had in him? The man holding him down put his elbow around his neck and jerked him off the bed. He heard a zipper pulling up as his attacker reared back and punched him in the stomach. Frank got into Malloy's face, and just whispered, "I know about the other room. This time it's your turn."

Part 9: Back to the Basement

The door at the bottom of the stairs creaked open as Luke stared at all the paraphernalia on the walls. There was dim light coming off the walls as his eyes adjusted. Frank came in behind them pushing away through the doorway. They paused, amazed at all the torture tools and devices they saw laid out before them. Frank took a deep breath. "There's some weird shit in here, man," he muttered as he took it all in. "Damn."

Luke turned to stare at the handcuffed man he just laid claim to. "So this is where you tortured my brother?" After fumbling for a light switch, he shoved Malloy into the room with the bondage table of floggers. What's more, Luke felt a twinge of anger; it was exactly what Brian described on the way to the house. The room was ripe with the scent of leather, with floggers, straps and other tools he had no comprehension of completely covering the walls. In the middle of the room, just where Brian said it would be, was a black leather padded table centered between four sturdy support posts, with power strips, chains and God knew what else on all sides. This is where he raped my little brother, he thought, staring at the overwhelming range of leather items surrounding the table. Tails of leather and rubber dangled from handles, suspended from wall hooks. Some handles were wrapped in woven leather latticework – some were layered wood. All looked menacing and capable of inflicting severe pain. Luke felt an urgent pulse of adrenaline shoot into his bloodstream. After his revenge fuck, beating the hell out of this guy was going to feel good.

Malloy remained silent, but was still resisting his captors. As Frank and Luke spun him around and tried to push him up on the table, he kicked out, but couldn't connect. Luke's arm plunged under the crook of Malloy's elbow and into the small of Malloy's back, forcing him to bend down in pain. "Get the cuffs off him," Luke ordered Frank. As Frank unlocked one wrist, Luke slapped it anew with the second pair of handcuffs. He grabbed the chain that hung off the ceiling, jerking Malloy's wrist up above his shoulder. Frank followed on the opposite side, spreading Malloy's arms out, cross-like between the chains. Malloy kept on with his struggling, so Frank double punched him in the diaphragm to knock his wind out.

As Malloy was gasping, Frank sneered at him, "You only pick on little people?" He and Luke dropped down to the leather ankle cuffs chained on the floor, strapping them across Malloy's ankles and stopping them from taking on his captors. Which he tried anyways, driving himself off balance. Luke and Frank answered with a volley of punches to his chest, bending him back over the edge of the bondage table. He later gasped at Frank, "You see how big the son of a bitch is?"

Luke gripped Malloy's face in a tight squeeze and pulled it up into his own. "So this is where you like to fuck people," he spat. Getting his gloved hands under Malloy's shirt collar, he jerked back hard and savored the satisfying rip of the cotton tearing apart. Frank took hold of the remaining tatters and pulled from behind the little more than white rags of cloth hanging off Malloy's arm.

For the first time, Luke and Frank got a look at the true size of the man they had captured and chained. Laced thick black chest hair covered a highly defined six-pack abdomen and a broad V-shaped iron muscled upper body. "He looks like fucking Hercules," Frank marveled. Malloy shot him a look of silent disgust.

That disgust sent Luke off. "This is for my brother, buddy," as he set off a fresh round of blows. "Understand that?" He and Frank rained punches into Malloy's chest and ribs, pummeling him until he was driven back down to the table. But the punches continued unabated, with Luke driving his fist into Malloy's packs and Frank landing strike after strike into his rib cage. Yet through it all, Malloy refused to give them little satisfaction other than grunts or shouts. "You had enough, punk boy," Luke leered as Malloy lay prone, gasping for breath. "You're a cop, you're supposed to be out protecting people," Frank snarled. "But you're down here fucking people!" He pulled back his arm to deliver several more jackhammer like hits to Malloy's gut. "It's party time, motherfucker," he declared watching as Luke stepped in to continue the punishing blows.

Luke finally took a pause. "Let's get him down from here and give him what he gives out." He decided, "Give me the key." Frank took the cuff key from his pocket and turned the lock open as Luke landed two more strikes to Malloy's rib cage. Malloy reflexively pulled his arm to his side, allowing Luke to pin it down and hold it, while Frank released the second cuff. Luke pushed his glove under Malloy's chin and squeezed his neck "I'm gonna torture you like you tortured my little brother," he promised. "Hold them, Frank."

Once they'd undone the ankle restraints, Luke signaled at Frank to get Malloy onto the bondage table. The two men spun their prisoner around, grabbing his arms and quickly hoisting him off the floor. Malloy landed with a hard bounce and slid up the black leather. Luke and Frank secured his wrists then made fast work of buckling the straps. Frank took particular delight in pulling the chest straps as tight as he could, chuckling as Malloy grunted at the pressure across his back. Luke stopped for a moment in the sudden realization of what he was doing. He looked at the hard muscled body he and Luke had captured, subdued, and in his case fuck dominated, and imagined what Brian felt when he was in the position of the cop.

The cop they'd just beaten into submission and was about to torture further. Even with his balls freshly drained, he felt a fresh surge growing. He took another look at the body he'd strapped, ass up, on the table. He felt the edge of his lip curl into a satisfied sneer. "That ass," he thought, "I own that ass now." He hissed at Malloy, "So this is what my brother felt like?"

Frank brought Luke back into concentrating on what they were doing in this hidden torture chamber when he saw Frank forcing Malloy, pulling back painfully on his neck, shouting into his face, "You like this, motherfucker? Huh? You fucking like this? Do you, punk bastard?"

The two men faced the wall of floggers and scanned for ones they thought would work. Luke reached for a black flogger with short tails on it, thinking it would be easy to swing. "Yeah, I like that," Frank said approvingly. Frank spotted a longer with long red tails, the color of which made him think of burning pain. He took that one off the wall and waved in the air. Luke was already beating Malloy when Frank let his first swing land across the tight muscles of their captive cop's ass. "Hey," Frank laughed, "I like that."

Luke was lashing away, barely taking a pause between hits. Frank was taking his time teasing the shins of his victim, mocking him between the swaying. "You like that, you like when it runs up your leg?" He taunted, letting the red leather tips trail at Malloy's leg before hauling back for a hard strike. A steady stream of cracks echoed in the cell, as Luke continued his aggressive attack, pounding on Malloy's back, thighs and ass, and raising angry red welts with each fresh hit.

Moving back up to Malloy's head, Frank wrapped the tails around Malloy's face and jerked the loop tight. "Did you put this shit into Brian's mouth like this?" He chuckled as the strands dug in Malloy's mouth. "Did you?" Yanking the flogger back, Frank pulled Malloy's head from side to side like he was holding on a horse's reins. He smiled at the sputtering grunts Malloy made, as Luke continued the beatings. Unwinding the flogger from Malloy's cheeks, he moved to the rear of the table and laid a cracking heave into Malloy's feet. That elicited the biggest yelp of the torture so far, and brought an even bigger smile to Frank's face.

Even Luke noticed that reaction, causing them to break from his torrent of lashes. "Remember what I told you about payback for my little brother?" Luke said into Malloy's ear. "Now you're going to pay, bitch." He looked up at Frank and nodded. "Go get Brian and bring him in. I'm not finished with this yet." He waited for Frank to leave the room and began hitting Malloy in the spots where he didn't see welts. He didn't want this punk to have a single, unmarked inch of skin left on him before he was finished. Luke savored each grunt from the body of their captive, even as he respected the toughness of a prisoner that had yet to utter a single word, despite the torture. He leaned in close, chest heaving from the exertion of flogging, to Malloy's face. "The deal is, now we're bringing my brother in."

Frank came around the doorway, with Brian right behind him. Malloy looked over, recognizing a little prick he'd caught hitchhiking the day before. But he also knew that if, as these two musclemen were claiming, this punk Brian had said he'd been fucked by him, it was a lie. Luke pulled Brian up to the head of the bondage bed and demanded, "Is this the guy?" Brian and Malloy stared at each other, Brian with a wicked sneer playing across his face. "Is this the guy that done that stuff to you?"

Luke waited until Brian nodded in agreement. Stepping between Brian and Malloy to look again and got in the face of their prisoner. "I am going to make you pay, you bastard."

Part 10: Comeuppance

Hearing this was the break that Malloy was waiting for. "I may have beaten your brother," he spat out, "but I didn't rape him."

Luke froze. The whole room went dead silent. Brian felt a chill go down his spine. If Brian knew anything, it was that his brother never trusted him. He also knew that getting caught in a lie would set Luke off in a very dangerous way. Brian felt Frank tense up behind him. Luke spun around to face Brian. "Is it true?" The flushed red face of his brother made Brian know that a storm was about to hit. "Is it true?"

The hesitation was all Luke needed to know. He and Frank were beating up a man based on Brian not telling them the truth. Strapped to the table, Malloy sensed the change in the wind. His captors bought it.

Frank grabbed Brian by the neck and shoved him face first next to Malloy. "You slimy little fuck," as he drove Brian face into the padding on the bondage table. "Do you have any idea what your brother did to this man?" While Luke was being driven into a rage, Frank was also boiling over with anger. Frank had seen his best friend brutally fuck another man with an insane sense of duty. And it was all based on a lie.

Before Brian could stop it, Luke had grabbed him, lifted him off the table by his neck, and pushed him towards the back of the room. "Did he even beat you? I put my dick up this man's ass because of what you told me. I just beat him black and blue, and you fucking lied to me all this time." Luke dropped his chokehold on Brian before punching him in the gut. There was an inversion bar hanging from the ceiling, and he picked up Brian turning him upside down. Frank came over and strapped Brian's ankles, leaving him dangling from the ceiling.

"You should know by now," barked Luke, undoing his belt, "you never lie to me." Frank followed Luke's lead, pulling his belt around his waist. Luke snapped his belt twice before leaning into his brother. "You little bitch. Now you're going to pay." Luke reared back and swung his double belt at Brian's stomach. Frank wasted no time in following up. Despite hanging upside down, Brian still doubled up in pain. But there was no escaping his punishment. Luke and Frank were acting in anger, and Brian knew there was nothing he could do about it.

The belts kept swinging as Brian swung above the floor, taking yet another beating in Malloy's prison. Blow after blow rained down across Brian's T-shirt, to the point where the fabric began to tear apart. Brian twisted and turned in the air, unable to avoid or stop the beating. Like before, when Malloy first had him tied up in this room, Brian began to feel a rush of endorphins pouring down the length of his body. He began to numb to the pain and began to float, not just from hanging by his ankles, but from the sensations racking his body. They build up and build up more, until once again Brian passed out.

Part 11: Afterwards

Out on the patio behind the house, Frank was yelling at Brian. Frank and Luke, still angry at Brian, had decreed that their boots be polished to a fine sheen. They had even allowed him to take off a T-shirt that they had ripped apart in their furious beating.

"What the hell are you doing? Put some muscle into it," Frank bellowed Brian. "It looks like you're using a Goddamn Hershey bar." Luke turned the corner along with Butch, the family Labrador.

"That's disgusting," Luke leered. "Can't you do if fucking thing right?" Butch took a good sniff around the boots before even he wandered off in disgust. "Even the dog thinks you're doing a shoddy job." Luke took a swing and cuffed Brian alongside his head. But then Brian heard another set of footsteps approaching.

When he looked up, it wasn't just Butch the dog but Malloy in full uniform, but just as much with the arrogant swagger he'd had when he first picked up Brian and at the cul-de-sac. "What the hell was he doing here," he whimpered.

Malloy smirked. He knew how to play Luke and Frank against Brian and against their own interests. Revenge would come for being raped in his own bed, but he was patient. He'd already beaten up the brother; the older sibling would take time. But he knew he could wait and his plan was set for the long haul.

"You lied to us," Luke responded, "so now I trust him more than I trust you."

Brian felt his balls draw up. Not only did his brother turn on him, he'd invited the very man who beat him unconscious into their house. He began to protest half-heartedly. But the three of his aggressors were having none of it. With Butch barking around the table and running in circles, Luke Frank and Malloy picked Brian up from the table, carried him over their heads, and threw him head over heels into the swimming pool. It was just one more piece of Brian's humiliation, and Malloy savored it.

With Brian treading water and fearful of climbing out of the pool, Malloy turned to Frank and Luke. Think of the long haul, he reminded himself. "You two are tough men," he said to Frank and Luke, playing off their arrogance. "I think I have a business idea for the three of us." When he saw their eyes light up, he knew his plan was off to a good start. *'The long haul,'* he thought again, *'the long haul. What a pair of dumbasses.'*

To be continued…

THE CANVAS

I pulled into the parking lot and heard the asphalt rolling underneath the tires. It was a long trip. My trusty hatchback, as usual, had plenty of art in the back covered with cloths, blankets, and tarps. The show seemed like a good idea; it was only a few hours away from where I live, so the cost for me was probably just registration, hotel, and some food. If I sold just three pieces of art, I would've made my money back. I was hopeful.

I parked the car, and went inside to the registration desk. It was obvious there were already plenty of kinky people there. But it was just as obvious that not everybody was kinky. It's kind of a rule at places like this: you don't approach people unless you really know what they're up to or in to. So I stepped up to the desk gave my name and registration info, and as I did, this handsome man sidled right up to me. While I didn't know him from Adam, he still stepped up and said, "Tell me boy, where will you be later?"

This was surprising, seeing as I didn't have any leather on, and had yet to even check in. But still I replied to him, "I'll be vending. I'm an artist and I have several paintings to put up on display."

"That's wonderful." He smiled at me again, and I could see the light dancing in his eyes. "I will look for you later," he said, "as I would really like to see what you paint."

I completed checking in and wheeled the cart, filled with my paintings, into the lobby area. The vendors had mostly set up and there was an area for me to hang several pieces of my work. The rest, including some drawings I had made earlier, I placed in a box on the table for better viewing. Most of them I'd covered in plastic so they wouldn't get damaged or smeared. Smaller works – which are easier to sell – were the ones that I had set aside. I also had some rough drawings I had not completed, mostly pen and ink, and some pencil.

I hid my suitcases under the table, and began hanging pictures along the walls and pillars of the vendor area. The market had yet to open, which meant I had plenty of time to make sure that everything was nicely displayed. The other vendors were busy hanging racks of leather, toys, and other assorted items. Most of the vendors were friends, as we all kind of make the same circuit when we sell. The Mart itself opened at one o'clock. A few of the vendors had picked up lunch, and behind their tables were eating and preparing for the onslaught of customers.

At one o'clock, the doors opened and attendees began to trickle in. Selling fetish artwork is a difficult proposition. Most customers at these kinds of events want toys or clothing. For the people that fly into events like this, a large piece of art is something they can't get on the airplane. For those that drive, one of my larger paintings is something they would have to put in the back of their car and be careful with while taking home. But again, because I was local, I only had to sell three items in order to make a profit this weekend. My hopes were pretty high.

About a half-hour into the market being opened, the gentleman I'd met at the front desk came up to my table. He looked around at the items hung along the wall, and some of the artwork in the box and portfolio. "You do really nice work," he said smiling. "I'd like to take at least two of these back with me."

I was quite surprised to hear that this early into the market. Most people wait until the very last minute to purchase artwork, and often the larger pieces don't sell at all. This man, who just walked up to me at the front desk and introduced himself vaguely, was going to make two thirds of my weekend in the first hour of the market being opened. I asked him which two pieces he really wanted. He pointed out first an oil painting I had done of a man straddling a tall boot. The bearer of the boot itself was not visible on the painting, but the very rich colors of the chaps of the man straddling it gave the picture depth. I felt a sense of pride, as I really believed that piece to be one of my better works.

The second one he wanted was of two men essentially forcing their way through a colored bubble, standing back to back, while slinging floggers. It was one of my more esoteric pieces. It was also one of the most expensive ones in the lobby. He asked me how much the total would be. When I told him, he didn't even bat an eye. "Can you take credit cards,?" he asked me.

"Of course I can," I replied. I had to introduce myself, and said, "My name is Jim. Jim Rhodes."

He took my hand and shook it firmly. "My name is Mikal," he said again flashing that smile.

As I wrote down his information, I asked him what he was going to do with the paintings he was purchasing. "I run a gay and lesbian library in Oklahoma," he said. "And I plan on putting these up in the gallery."

Frankly, I was stunned. Not just stunned, but deeply flattered. Most people took my items and put them up in their bedrooms or in their dungeons or play spaces. To be on display in the library was an honor that I did not expect. I finished taking down his payment information, and quickly rifled through my rough drawings. I found a pen and ink drawing of two men locked in a passionate embrace. Although it was very much homage to Tom of Finland, I still thought it would be nice to give this to this man. I took a blue sharpie marker, and signed it "To Mikal, with deepest appreciation. Jimmy." I helped him take the two pictures down from their display area, and carefully wrapped them with tissue and bubble wrap. I took a manila folder, and inserted the pen and ink drawing.

"Jimmy," he said firmly, "what do I owe you for the extra picture."

I waved my hand away, to indicate that this was a gift. Mikal had pretty much already made my weekend a half-hour into the show. Giving him an extra drawing seemed like the least I could do.

He accepted the manila folder from my hands. "That is very generous of you." And without missing a beat, he added, "Tell me, Jimmy, are you a whipping bottom?"

Well, I thought, that was pretty forward. I hesitated for a moment. Master Mikal seemed so guileless. There was something genuinely inviting and enticing about him and his approach seemed more like destiny than just some kind of pickup. He also had a complete command of the situation, almost like it would be rude to say no. "Yes sir, I have been."

"Oh, good," he said. Leaning in with just a hint of conspiratorial cheer, he continued, "How far."

This time, I didn't hesitate. "I've been whipped till I've been bleeding."

He clapped his hands together, and held them there. "Very good. When the vendor Mart closes, I'd like very much to beat you."

There was such buoyancy in his request that I simply smiled and nodded my head yes. I told him that I had yet to unpack, but would get to his room as soon after seven o'clock as I could. "I'll be looking for you, Jimmy," he replied as he turned with his paintings and drawing, striding away.

When seven o'clock finally came around, I was high as a cloud. In addition to the sales I had made to Master Mikal, I sold another small painting to another attendee. In just a few hours, I had covered my cost for the event. As I politely urged the stragglers to leave the lobby, I really felt eager to serve. I pulled the handle up for my suitcase, closed and locked the lobby doors behind me, and headed for the elevators. To my surprise, Master Mikal was standing at the elevator doors waiting for me. "Sir, I was on my way up to see you. I'd like to unpack, and take a shower before I come to your room, if that is okay with you."

He took my suitcase from my hand. "You will shower and change in my room, Jimmy," he stated with authority. "I've been looking forward to this since I saw you at registration."

So he had been scoping me out. Nothing wrong with that, I thought. Actually, it felt very complimentary. We boarded the elevator, and he punched the eighth floor. Master Mikal was staying in one of the hotel's suites. "You won't need to unpack just yet," he said, "You'll be naked anyway. Go take that shower, Jimmy."

It felt good to soap up and wash off. It was a long drive to get here and several hours of working in the lobby. Plus, this man made me feel very welcome. I toweled myself off, and stepped out of the bathroom. Master Mikal had donned his black leather cowboy hat, and a black leather vest. There were two large cases on one of the beds, with one open. Master Mikal beckoned me to the side of the bed where he was sitting. "Kneel here, Jimmy," he commanded. "I want you to get a sense of what we'll be doing tonight."

I knelt between the beds in front of Master Mikal. First, he picked up a wispy, soft leather flogger, with long tails. "This is what I will use to warm you up." He held it up to my lips, and I kissed it. He picked up a second flogger, this one with thicker tails, and a heavier handle. "This one, I will use to make your back red." Resting the handle against my lips, I kissed that one as well. The third flogger was far more severe looking. The tails were braided leather, each with the knot at the end. "I will use this one to hurt you," he said, allowing the braids to drape over my head and face. He drew the flogger back, sliding the braids up and over my forehead. The next item was a single tail whip that looked to be about 4 feet long. He coiled it around my neck, placing the handle between my lips. I held it there as he said, "This one will be the one that leaves marks."

I knew that there was one more item on the bed, but Master Mikal had been shielding it from me. He uncoiled the single tail from around my neck, and from the bed withdrew a long, black bullwhip. The length of it snaked back along my spine to the floor. He rested his hand against my cheek as he said "And this one is the one that will finish you off." Deliberately, he let the leather of the bullwhip withdraw up my shoulder, which made me shudder. Standing, he laid the bullwhip back on the bed. "Jimmy, I need to know that you trust me. Tell me, do you?"

He tucked his hand under my chin and lifted me to a standing position. "Yes sir," I replied, "I offer you my absolute trust." He took my hand and guided it to the ceiling-high post of one of the beds. Artfully, he rope-cuffed my wrist into place. Without a word, he bound the second one. He ran his hands down my back, allowed them to cup my ass. My body now stretched against the wall; I realized, maybe for the first time, that Master Mikal was probably only as tall as my shoulder. But he exuded such confidence and charisma that I thought originally he towered over me.

I felt the first, soft brushes of that flogger he'd shown me initially. In a hushed voice, he told me "Jimmy, this is where we begin our journey." With a steady rhythm, the strokes continued. I could feel the early heat, the rushing blood, rising to the skin of my shoulders. Master Mikal was giving me a gentle, caressing opening shot. "You're a good boy, Jimmy," he murmured, "just ride with me." I sucked in a huge gasp of air as the first round of flogging suddenly stopped. Master Mikal ran his fingertips across the broad area that he had been hitting. I felt that goose bumps feeling, coolness meeting warmth.

I saw him lay the flogger down across the bed and pick up the thicker tailed, second instrument. He rubbed himself against my back, gently pushing me into the wall. "Let's continue," as he backed away from my body. I felt the wash of air as Master Mikal judged the distance between his arm, his flogger, and my back. The harder, heavier strips of leather were soon applying their pressure from his well-targeted swings.

My shoulders took each thump and thud as he increased the intensity. I could hear his breathing in rhythm with his strokes. I tried to breathe in time with the sound of his.

What felt like warmth a few minutes ago now felt like heat. He stopped flogging me, tossed the flogger onto the bed, and again rushed and pressed against my back. I shook, his body again pressing me against the wall. He reached over, picking up the braided cat and coiled it around my neck. "Jimmy," he whispered, "do you know why you need this?"

I could feel Master Mikal breathing against the burning in my shoulders and back. The endorphins were already rushing through my body. And despite the hushed tone of his voice, it was easy to sense his excitement. "Yes Sir, Master Mikal, and I am honored to give it to you."

"Oh Jimmy, Jimmy," as he withdrew the cat from around my face, "you are such a good boy." I sturdied myself against the wall, knowing that the next hits would hurt deeply. "Are you ready to go deep?" he asked me. I nodded my head down in preparation. This time there was no practice swing, and knots struck me like tiny leather ball bearings. For the first time that evening, I cried out. Behind me, I could hear Master Mikal inhale with a sense of accomplishment. But he did not let up. Blow after blow rained down across my shoulders, my back, my ribs, with swings that cut up from the back of my thighs and across the cheeks of my ass. As he had not struck my ass until now, the pain was like an eruption. Breathing in rhythm was now a chore. But I could feel my body responding to each sting of each braided tail. The knots dug into my skin, exposing me to Master Mikal and his desires. My gasps were now individual yelps. The room began to feel smaller, Master Mikal closer, the world outside oblivious. Time no longer registered. So when Master Mikal placed the braided cat back on the bed, I leaned into the wall, swallowing the air. He held the short whip from my elbow across the wall to my other elbow. He blew cool breaths across the area that the knots had broken open. But this time he whispered something that took me completely by surprise. "Tell me, Jimmy," as he continued to blow air across the wounds, "do you know why I need this?"

I felt my brain just expand inside the bubble that now encased us. I felt him back away, and heard the first crack of his whip. He cracked it again to get my attention, before the first blow sliced into my shoulders. I no longer was yelping, this time I screamed.

"Good boy Jimmy, good boy," Master Mikal exalted, "take what you need!"

There is no way to know what kind of pace Master Mikal was using with his whip. All I could feel was the rise in my skin. The crack of the air. The sound of Master Mikal telling me I was his good boy. The pain continuing to spread, rising throughout my body into my mind. Then one crack struck me and tore me apart. I screamed to shatter the air, and slumped into the wall. I could see the walls moving as Master Mikal came up behind me. He began to stroke my skin, speaking suggestively and calmly as I gasped for breath against the wall. I pulled myself up in his ropes as he spoke. "I think we have reached your limits," he said to me.

Still gasping for breath, I responded "Yes sir, thank you, sir." The room was coming back into focus, and I could still feel the intensity swirling around us. "Thank you, sir, thank you, sir." I repeated again.

"You're such a good boy, Jimmy," he said with a satisfied tone. "But we are not done. Take five more."

It was then that I remembered the long bullwhip he'd shown me. I began to feel tears in my eyes, knowing that there were at least five more hard hits to come. I remembered how long that whip felt hanging across my shoulders and down my back. There was an unsubtle whoosh of air as Master Mikal judged the distance. "Here is your first, Jimmy."

With that, the first circle of an inferno raged across my body. I clamped my teeth shut, trying not to tear the bed down. The second and third blows came in rapid succession, crossing each side of my back. "That's three, Jimmy," I heard him say.

The air hissed above my head. I braced myself, sobbing, for the last two strikes. The first felt like a long metal spike was plunged into my shoulder and torn out. I know I screamed, but I barely recognized the sound. Before I had even finished crying out, the final blow landed with equal force on my opposite shoulder. This time, I slumped in the bonds, sobbing uncontrollably. Master Mikal immediately came up behind me, wrapping his arms around me, and murmured, "You're a good boy, Jimmy. You're a very good boy."

I soon heard the click of the other case on the bed, and Master Mikal withdrew a large, stunning, silver saber. He slipped it under the ropes that bound my wrists to the bedposts, cutting me free. His strength eased me face down onto the bed. He had taken his shirt off, and I could see the spots of my blood on his chest. His face was glowing, and there was an energy between us. An energy that felt like we were flying. Master Mikal was caressing my shoulders as I lay there; the sobbing subsiding. This was a special session with a genuinely unique Dominant. In that moment, I had an inspiration that would save this time in each of our memories.

As Master Mikal continued to rub my shoulders and back, talking me down. I asked him a special request. "Sir, will you please do me a favor."

"And what would that be, Jimmy?"

"Sir, I'd like you to take the drawing that I signed for you today, and press it into my back." I felt his hands freeze, his touch locked in place. There was a long pause before he finally spoke. "Jimmy," he said breathlessly, "that would mean more to me than you can possibly imagine."

He moved away from the bed, and opened the envelope that I had placed the drawing in earlier. Returning to the foot of the bed, he sized up the area that he had beaten. He adjusted his position, and pressed the paper first into my left shoulder then into my right. As he lifted the piece away, he said in a whisper, "Look up, boy."

When I turned my head to look up at the picture, there were two bright red streaks above my signature. I glanced towards Master Mikal, and realized that there were tears in his eyes. I also knew that this session was as special for him as it was for me.

After a long period of holding each other and returning to Earth, I asked him about the sword. When I think of sketches, I have a mental image in my head. When I saw Master Mikal pick up the sword with the scabbard in one hand, and the tip braced into his palm, in my mind a broad outline of him, the silver of his goatee, and the buoyancy of his expression, his leather vest and black hat immediately filled my mind like a sketchpad. He swung the sword in the air, almost as if he was dancing with it.

"I love to whip," he said with pride, "but blades are my true passion." He lowered the tip of the sword towards my face and I involuntarily shuddered. "Jimmy, did I scare you?"

My mental sketchpad once again filled with the image of Master Mikal dancing with the saber in the hotel room. I knew that once I got home I would be transferring this image to paper or canvas. "Sir, I have never been able to get past a fear of knives to play with anyone who loves them."

Master Mikal's eyes lit up. "Never?" he asked. I nodded in the affirmative. "Oh, Jimmy, Jimmy," he smiled. "Oh, Jimmy." He withdrew the sword, laying it back in its case. But in each hand now was a pair of bayonets. "I want to be the first."

I looked at that beaming face, the command in his eyes, and knew trust. Certainly not this weekend, probably not this month, maybe not even this year. But as my mind's eye again filled with the sight of Master Mikal dancing with his saber, and the look of undiluted joy as he and I looked at the bloodstain on the drawing, I knew that someday Master Mikal would be drawing his blades across my flesh.

I could only hope that by the time we met again, I will have finished his portrait.

ANDROID POLICE

"The more complex man's inventions become, the more creative will be his perversions."

– From a memo by Dr. Joseph Melinki, Director and CEO of the PSA division of Android Research Assemblage, during initial market research for the PS (personal service) 9400 androids, Feb 14, 2062.

Police Report. Robotics corrections: Case 1267. March 23. 2066. Injury and damage assessment.

Officer Michael Brownbode was attacked by a trio of Personal Service Androids Appox: 10:45 PM outside the Perimeter of Cyprus College. When Officer Brownbode approached an erratically acting android, he began giving standard tests to see if the android was renegade. While questioning the suspect, two other androids overpowered Officer Brownbode and struck him with their hands about the head, chest, and groin. After Officer Brownbode was knocked to the ground, one of the androids kicked him in the ribs and leg.

This is very atypical of personal service androids, which have as one of their primary priorities of manufacturer's orders to never harm a human being.

Officer Brownbode was transported to Mercyhurst Hospital for treatment of two broken ribs and a fracture in his left upper leg. Both injuries resulted from kicks sustained during the attack.

Due to these injuries, Officer Brownbode will be assigned to a vehicle, and not foot patrol. Effective immediately, he is to be assigned a full-size Robotics Patrol truck.

Internal Memo. From the Board of Directors of Android Research Assemblage. To Dr. Joseph Melinki. April 30, 2066.

Joseph: FOR YOUR EYES ONLY!

We have received several accounts of PS 2400's forming packs after turning renegade. This much has been confirmed: Although the fail-safe mechanism will defeat an android being reprogrammed by anyone but its owner, we had to look into the alternate possibilities. Even if, as originally postulated, one android cannot reprogram another, we did not take into account that more than two androids could reprogram each other, one by one. What we have discovered is that since the packs tend to be trios, when one robot turns renegade, he will locate two other robots, one for him to reprogram, and the third to reprogram the second, and then each "fine-tunes" the other. It defeats the program that disables a second robot's ability to reprogram the first and complete the initial reprogramming, by passing the duties around a circle of other androids.

This programming error must be corrected immediately. As of this time, no recalls are planned.

Police report. Robotics corrections:
Case 1301. January 5, 2067.

There were two cases of Robotic Mutilations reported during the night. First report was at 9:45 PM, the second at 10:05 PM. Both Robots were PS9400 models; both were discovered on the Plains Park Waterway, Downtown Houston. Both were damaged beyond repair. The primary damage to each was a hole to the head portions. Other damage included tearing and removal of the android's poly-skin covering in several areas, indicating signs of struggle and evasive action. The damaged PS9400 models were sent to labs for further investigation.

Lab Report. Reference to Robotics Corrections:
Case 1301. January 7, 2067.

Upon our investigation, it has been determined that the two model PS9400 robots were not terminated by a gunshot, as previously suspected. The hole to each robot was delivered by the same instrument. Further inspections reveal that the piercings have a spiral groove that would make it inconsistent with a bullet twist, and the circumference was a near perfect circle. A bullet would show signs of impact that would (normally) leave a less than perfect perimeter. These wounds were more in accordance with a power tool. We suspect a hand drill was used in the termination of both of these models. The abrasive tears in the poly-skin indicate skin-slashing strikes, and appear to be inflicted by some kind of knife.

Police report. Robotics corrections: Case 1359. October 29, 2067.

Another reported Android Mutilation of a PS9400 model was recorded at approximately 12:25 AM. Although prior terminations of the 9400 models have shown escalated acts of brutality, this is the most severe. The android was found near the oil pipelines near the Old Canal Borough Townhouse development tracts. There were no markings as in other previous six cases of a power drill termination. There again were markings on the android's appendages of abrasions and tearing to the poly-skin, denoting apparent forcible restraint; glue residue may indicate that some kind of adhesive tape may have been used. There were also indications that damages inflicted on this particular android were not committed to cause termination, but to stimulate sensory pain/warning sensors to the neural net. As with all androids released from the PS9400 and on, if the warning sensors receive too much or prolonged stimuli, the main drive will automatically wipe itself and destroy its occupant's ability to have memory accessed as a security measure to the original owner of the contract. Only the original owner can reprogram the broad operational functions, and only the manufacturers (in the case of the PS9400, Android Research Assemblage) can terminate an android but also recover the original memory and motor skills. Additional damage to this case included burn marks across the android's upper body area, hands and feet (size of the burnings would indicate use of a cigarette or cigar), abrasions across the backside of the android (consistent with a belt or strap), and damage to the auditory receptions (narrow, sharp object insertions). Our conclusion is that, were this victim human instead of android, the determination would be that the victim had been tortured to death.

Notice of this crime has been forwarded to federal authorities, Android Research Assemblage, and the Behavior Psychological Division. The BPD has promised us a full psychiatric profile as soon as possible.

E-mail. Behavior Psychological Division.
Pertaining to: Robotics corrections: Case 1359.
October 31, 2067.

Gentlemen,

It is likely that the alleged "PSKiller" (Don't you love those tabloids?) will be a white male, between 35 and 45, and single. His escalated anger at his targets probably stems from a feeling of superiority over a machine he feels impinges on his definition of unreal against the real (robots vs. Mankind). There will likely be some kind of violent incident in his far past (possibly childhood abuse), or something more recent, which would point to his animosity towards robots, and the human appearance of personal androids in particular. Your worries that he will switch from mechanical to human victims is unfounded, as this guy gets his kicks from destroying the "superior mind" of a "subhuman" victim and would consider acts of sadism against a person beneath contempt. Also look for an authority figure, self-confidence bordering on cocky, and possibly a man displaced in a job by, or in direct cause of, an android. All information aside, we have never encountered this kind of criminal activity before, and wish to be kept in the loop on this case.

November 17, 2067.

"Freeze, Robot! Identify!"

The android turned and went into safe-stance, feet wide, hands apart, fingers flat together. Its signal lights strobed in compliance to code, and it transmitted "PS9400, registered to Mr. James Baker, 1736 Highlands Road, Houston, Texas, Officer Sir," as regulations asserted. This didn't satisfy the officer, who was camouflaging himself in the darkness of the freeway overpass. Thunder from the trucks overhead made it hard to read the android's audio response, so the android moved to step into the light and make himself more observable.

There was a slight crunch as the officer appeared. He was short, stocky and with a suggestion of a limp. The flashlight in front of his body kept his face hidden. "Step up to the van, robot," the officer ordered. The android easily recognized the symbols and bar coding of a member of Robotics Corrections, as all robots are programmed to upon manufacture. He walked to the open rear doors of the commanding officer's vehicle, but the officer blocked entry and shone the flashlight into the android's eye receptors. "I detect a tremor in the visual receptions on this one," the officer reported into the deck of the vehicle's data voice recorder. "About to run the standard non-citizen detection checklist." The officer lowered his flashlight just long enough to allow the robot to enter the van. But before the officer began to ask any questions, the android detected a sensor transmission block at the base of its neck pivot. The officer had thrown Gummah Insul across the transmitting patch.

The officer dropped his flashlight long enough to wrap duct tape around the android's feet and hand appendage areas, and just as quickly forced a fluid insertion tube down the intake in the android's mouth area. The android didn't understand the conflicting nature of the actions as per requirements of protocol programming, and as it tried to internal memo its hard disc of Robotics Corrections staff files, scalding water was forced down the intake to sear the vocalization module.

As with any sign of internal damage, automatic pain warning sensors fired a static jolt to the android's main neural net. But with the tape negating motion to help, the android could only emit an electronic squealing scream as the water destroyed its ability to vocalize.

The officer narrowed the distance between sweat forming at the tips of his moustache and the android's faceplate, and sneered, "Do you know what I like about androids that can't deactivate the pain sensors?" He was forcing a small thin blade between the android's skullcap and the memory retention recorder, and finished his question. "The fucking screams they make while I fuck with the pain sensors' cut-off point. You're about to go off line, you inhuman stack of tin."

The android was in the center of the search answer and was trying to record the data when the blade disengaged the hard disc connections to the recorder. "Robotic Correction Badge Number 2006, Sgt. Officer, motor vehicle unit, Mi…"

The connection was broken there.

HOUSTON CHRONICLE ARTICLE.
November 19, 2067.

SIXTH VICTIM FOUND IN PSKILLER ANDROID SPREE

The individual known only as the Personal Service Killer is believed to be the culprit behind the vandalization of a sixth robot. The latest destruction took place under an overpass in the Highlands' warehouse district. Although local authorities are keeping tight lipped about these incidents, they will admit to a pattern of similar android destructions. A source from outside the bureau claims each of the androids were PS9400's, and from incidents thereon, have shown that androids were restrained and violently brutalized, forcing their security devices against their main programs to crash and delete all programming. Initially used to protect the security of the owners, it effectively renders the android useless, not re-programmable, and leaves old memory unobtainable. When questioned about these descriptions, a high-ranking official of Robotics Corrections replied that there was no way to determine if the attacks were systematic in their destructive intent.

Charges against the person responsible for these acts would include grand larceny, and illegal robot termination.

Internal Memo. From the Board of Directors. To all staff of Android Research Assemblage. November 28, 2067.

Staff: We now have a crisis on our hands. PS9400 sales have dropped dramatically since the incidents of the PSkiller crimes have become more widely reported.

Officials in Robotic Corrections are asking us to program several 9400's with a recoverable memory that will not wipe if the android is accosted. The request is for five; I think it pertinent to manufacture more. We have until Friday, and I need to emphasize that, literally, our future is on the line. There will be a 5000-credit bonus for the team that successfully creates the program.

December 1, 2067.

The Robotics Corrections van was parked near the base of the park entrance, but the three robots had determined the officer was not nearby. They had turned renegade four days ago and had managed to avoid detection. The trio headed to the main gate of the park, hoping to find a secure place to spend the night. But as they neared the iron gate bars, another Robotics Correction van hit them with high-beamed headlights, and the stunned robots turned to face an Officer armed with an automatic stun shot. They had already turned off their internal messaging recorders in order to avoid radio transmission detection, so there was no chance to notify authorities of their situation. All the androids could see was the cherry red flaring of the officer's cigar in the dark; it was the last thing they recorded before the stun shot put each android in a state of temporary shutdown.

Residence of Sgt. Officer John Brownbode.
Early morning. December 2, 2067.

He looked at his three latest conquests, each strapped and secured in different vulnerable positions. The silver duct tape struck a nice contrast to the color of the artificial flesh tones. He stood for a few minutes, just gazing across the room at his new victims. This was what he had waited for all this time: a pack of renegades, just like the dirt holes that had left him crippled barely a year ago. Officer Mike Brownbode had plans for this bunch.

The androids had deprogrammed their citizen protocols and were threatening Officer Brownbode. Brownbode looked at them, cursing and struggling. "God, you tin scraps curse like sailors. I bet Android Research never thought you'd learn to swear, but even a parrot can curse. That damn robot chatter, nothing but a bunch of damned mimic birds! They never could make you talk like a man. I am sick of listening to it... and I have a hot pan full of lead to feed you." Brownbode forced a mouth insertion into each of his prisoner's intakes. "Care for a drink?" He poured a trickle of molten metal down each android's throat and watched with glee as, one by one, the androids' pain sensors forced them into a back-arching sensory reflex. The vocalization mechanisms were now melted down enough to allow little more than shrieking scream-like emissions. Brownbode chuckled. "That's the only sound I want from my androids," he said. "Give me a few minutes and you won't be able to hear each other, either."

Brownbode produced three ordinary wood kabob skewers and probed the android's audio receptor inserts with a deliberate slowness. As he jammed the point into the androids' "eardrum" devices, Brownbode watched as the pain sensors began making the robots fight to minimize the damage. "Sorry plastic freaks…you don't get to hear each other scream. But you, you're the ringleader. You get to hear me tear your buddies apart, and get a real good idea what's coming to you. What do you think about that?"

The alpha bot could only screech in reply as he heard the first android squealing in defense. Officer Brownbode scratched away at the eardrums until neither of the followers in this renegade crew was able to understand the sounds of what was occurring in Officer Brownbode's garage. Master Brownbode picked up a circular sander from his tool bench and pressed it against the first android's footpads. "Hey boss brain," he called over to the lead android. "Think he'll have heels after this?" The android, unable to cease function of its visual receptors, was forced to observe as Officer Brownbode began shredding the imitation flesh coating from the first android's feet. It tore away like frog skin. The android's pain warning systems were reaching maximum capacity when Officer Brownbode eased off the power sander. As he waited for the systems to return to operational, he laughed at the lead bot. "How about this one? Think I should shred his pants?"

Brownbode went to the second android and jammed the power sander into the crotch of the second's bot-levis. "Think this kind of pain could overload him?" Brownbode set the sander to low speed and let the denim disintegrate below the circular spins of the sandpaper, and then the artificial skin of the android's liquid waste outlet. Brownbode laughed as he shouted, "Anatomically correct? You can't jack off! You can't come! You can't even get a hard on unless you're programmed to! But a MAN can! Don't matter how much they try and make you better… you'll always be nothing better than a smart toaster; you fucking freaks!"

Smoke was starting to come off the android's pants and poly-skin when Officer Brownbode stopped the sander. "He's got to cool off. I'll get back to your other buddy soon. Too bad they can't hear each other scream. But I know you can, and that's fine with me."

The lead android was thrashing about in the duct tape and chains, as all sectors of its programming diverted to defense. The electronic tones generated from the systems of his trio were alarms of eminent termination, as their warning sensors were reaching their limits before protective information wipes and cessation of mechanical functions. He observed as the Officer picked up a large power tool and held it by the front plate of the third android and switched it on. It began to glow bright red and the alpha bot identified the tool as a soldering iron.

"I think I'll send the rest of you tin punks a message," Brownbode snarled at him. His knife cut away the second android's shirt as Brownbode touched the chest area of the android's poly-skin. A searing sound and thick stench rose off as Officer Brownbode spoke aloud the words he was branding into the android's skin. "I… am… less than… sub-… human." He laughed as the android began its electronic wail at the first word and as the robotic appendages began flailing and twisting.

"I… am… man-made… shit."

The alpha bot could hear the subtle change in the emergency tone, and realized time was eminent, even if the officer could not. Then the tone changed audibly as the android gave one last jerk, the mechanical program going off line, and the microsecond pulse of a complete memory wipe.

"Too bad for your pal there," Officer Brownbode whispered to the alpha bot. "I'm tired, and want to go to bed. Gotta work tomorrow, you know. There's got to be a few more other pisskay's to trash. Let's make it a race, huh?" Brownbode picked up the second android and set it on a table saw, and then wrapped a metal collar about the alpha bot's neck pivot. He pulled the length of the chain back to a winch on the wall, and turned the hand crank till there was no slack. "I never took a robot's head off before, so let's see which works faster. I'll bet the table saw, but you never know, do you?" Brownbode took his belt off and dropped his pants. As he switched both tools to on, he began stroking his erect cock to the sounds of mechanical tools and mechanical screams. The second android began to push into the blade as the alpha bot began pulling tight against the table. Brownbode puffed hard on his cigar, beating his cock, watching as each screaming android's head tore off the bodies. He shot his load with a howl as the heads flew across the garage floor.

He stood in a thick cloud of smoke till he recovered enough breath to shut down the saw and winch. The android head closest to him, he kicked into the opposite wall and laughed. "What do you know. Both heads came off at once." Officer Brownbode hit the lights as he exited the garage and chuckled. "Ain't science wonderful?"

Android Research Assemblage, Research and
Developmental Programming. December 4, 2066.

Tom Goodman brushed a stack of Whopper wrappers away from his legal pad, and drew a red ink line from one line of code to the next. As he leaned conspiratorially towards his cubicle partner David Mannon, he could feel the anger rising as he struggled to keep his voice down. "Did you hear that the cops recovered three more PS9400's," he whispered, "with their heads ripped off? They didn't release this to the papers, but whatever sick fuck has been trashing them PS's has been pouring lead in their mouths and shredding their balls off."

"Tom," Dave replied, "androids don't have balls."

Internal Memo. From the Board of Directors.
To all staff of Android Research Assemblage.
December 5, 2067.

Thanks to the extra hard work of Tom Goodman and David Mannon, we now have a six-android fleet of "undercover" androids prepared to deploy as decoys. Goodman and Mannon will both receive the promised 5000-credit bonus and the company both thanks and congratulates them for their diligent work at this very important time in ARA's history.

Old Canal District, Houston.
December 8, 2067. "Freeze, Robot, identify!"

Pack A of the ARA reprogrammed androids fell to safe stance formation as the stocky officer wandered towards them, the smoke from his cigar drifting behind him. The flickering of streetlamps had just begun negating the shadows of the lowering sun, and the video-receptors of the undercover PK's began recording the Officer's actions. When he gruffly commanded the androids to enter the Robotics Corrections van, they began their protocol checks, but also began transmitting the Officer's badge number and the license plate number of the vehicle for a positive match. "Robotic Correction Badge Number 2006, Sgt. Officer, motor vehicle unit, Michael Brownbode." The information was current, but then Officer Brownbode produced a roll of adhesive tape and secured one of the android's ankle appendages. When the officer attempted to smear Gummah Insul across the lead android's transmitting patch, their reserve programming was activated.

To the surprise of Officer Brownbode, the two androids he had not yet restrained threw themselves at him and forced him to the floor of the truck. As the two androids held Brownbode down, the third tore away the ankle tape and used Brownbode's handcuffs to restrain him. Shouts of "Not again, goddam it, not again," were recorded from the android transmission. Then, inexplicably, the transmissions were discontinued.

Android Research Assemblage, Research and Developmental Programming. December 4, 2066.

"Tom," Dave replied, "androids don't have balls."

Tom's faced flushed red. "That's not the fucking point, now is it? This bastard is torturing them like that have balls! He whupped them with a goddam belt! If somebody got caught doing that to a dog, he'd be locked up for life. Here it's just considered theft of property." He drew another angry red line across his code pad. "I got that memory save the company wants figured out. But I need you to help me get a few bonus lines in."

Dave leaned into Tom this time. "What do you mean, 'bonus lines'?"

There was a dark chuckle from Tom. "I've been working on the codes for PKs since I started working here. These are my babies, man. Nobody fucks up my babies...

Old Canal District, Houston. December 8, 2067.

"Not again, God dammit, not again!" the officer screamed as the androids pinned him down and handcuffed his wrists behind his back. The android pulled the back van doors closed as the Officer continued to struggle underneath the weight of the remaining two androids. He took the duct tape that had been used to tape his appendages and slapped a strip across the mouth of Officer Brownbode, who was beginning to flush bright red with fear. As the two androids holding him to the ground pulled back, one picked up the still-lit cigar from the floor of the van and jammed it into the skin of Brownbode's exposed forearm. The soundproofing of the van contained the wail of pain, but the stench of Brownbode losing control of himself filled the van.

Try as Brownbode could to cry for help, the duct tape held any noise inside the van he'd used to imprison other androids over the last year. Brownbode could feel the burning sear of hot ash in his arm as he uncontrollably relieved himself. He flashed back to the night barely a year ago when he lay on the ground, trying to curl into a protective position as steel-toed kicks were crashing into his ribs and legs. But this time was different. The androids were being deliberate. They had to know that a lit cigar was going to hurt more than harm him, and why the gag?

The lead android pulled the thin knife Brownbode had used to slice through the memory transmission cables from Brownbode's shirt pocket. Lodging it under the Officer's pants leg, he slit the pants open to the waist, and then did likewise to the opposite leg. Then, he repeated the action to Brownbode's soiled boxers. With the officer lying bare-assed and smelling like shit, the android ripped the duty belt from the sliced off uniform pants and tore the Officer's accoutrements away. The two accomplice androids pinned Brownbode back down on the floor of the van again, and the lead android began silently, methodically cracking the thick belt back and forth across Brownbode's ass.

Brownbode felt the explosions beginning after the two PK's began holding him down. As hard as he struggled, there was just no way he was strong enough to fight off two machines. Trapped to the ground, he could only scream with each successive strike of his duty belt. The androids were showing no mercy in their punishment, and Brownbode could feel the skin of his ass firing up. His vessels were bursting and flooding his skin with purple blood marks, and the swelling was excruciating. The lashing continued without letup, one clock-like blow landing with the exact same force as the last. And the next, over and over. Brownbode was no longer trying to scream for help, the cries were now nothing more than involuntary agony.

Just as suddenly, the belt whipping stopped. The two androids didn't let up on their pressure, and Brownbode gasped and whimpered, his cheeks red, puffing in and out as he tried to regain his breath. Tears were streaming down his face and he could feel the heat of blood running across his hips from the non-stop beating the android had delivered. Brownbode's mind was swirling, conflicted. Anger, horror, terror...and ultimately defeat and humiliation. For a second time, these machines that he loathed and hated more than anything on earth had gotten the better of him, trapping him in his own van and using him as nothing more than a punishment dummy. He tried again to shake his captors off, but it was a futile gesture. Debased and humiliated, he began to just cry like a beaten cat.

The android had stopped thrashing the Officer's ass and dropped the belt. It clicked into another new program that had been uploaded prior to its deployment, and began scanning the contents of the van. A bottle of water, a hose, a length of chain, a stun pole...and stopped when it identified a billy club. Reaching across his android accomplices, he lifted the club above Brownbode's back, just as the history in his programming instructed.

Android Research Assemblage, Research and Developmental Programming. December 4, 2066.

Dave leaned into Tom this time. "What do you mean, 'bonus lines'?"

There was a dark chuckle from Tom. "I've been working on the codes for PKs since I started working here. These are my babies, man. Nobody fucks up my babies, motherfucker. Back in 1997, there was a case when some NYPD cops sodomized a Haitian immigrant with a broom handle or something? According to the LEO library, it was something about 'Giuliani Time.' If I have to make my androids play bad cop, I am going to make them play really bad motherfucking cop…"

Old Canal District, Houston. December 8, 2067.

There was some kind of activity going on behind him, but the androids pinning him down were blocking his eyes from seeing past the floor of the van. Just as suddenly, he felt a force against his shit covered asshole. Even the gag across his face couldn't withhold the scream as the lead android forced his billy club inside his hole… deeper and deeper. Brownbode could feel his guts churning, as the android paused for just a mere second, dragging the club out an inch or two, and repeating the violation a second and third time. As he felt the muscles in his ass ripping apart and the lightning stabs of pain tearing into his gut, the only thing Brownbode could do was lie, whimpering and crushed, through his final humiliation at the hands of the PS9400's.

THE MOST IMPORTANT RIGHT NOW

He hovered over the man on the cross, frustrated, massive shoulders heaving for breath. The frustration came from seeing the boy's body, limp with the pain but flying on the endorphins, seeing the face of the great slave god and not sharing that vision with the guide who took him to the portal.

A wild inner animal raged within. "Now now… let me see what this boy sees now," roared inside his head. More than a small amount of effort had to be exerted in self-restraint; the anger was so erratically destabilized. There was danger lurking just behind the impulse to swing his whip one more time, and wipe the fucking serenity from that boy's face.

"Damn it, I need to feel it, please God, why can't I know what this man can?" All he knew is that, not so long ago, he was skilled enough a Master to be a co-passenger in these visions. He would bring a sobbing man back to earth from the cross, sobbing himself, tears of ecstatic happiness.

Not anymore. Instead of visions, voids. In place of the ecstasy, animal fury. In the space where joy used to emerge, a lid had to be clamped on the dangerous pressure cooker of pure unbridled sadism... pain for pain's sake. The welts he laid before would forge two men to one spirit and one vision, the warm blood forever tying them to a lifetime memory of a vision shared. Now the question nagged him... from where and when did these failures originate?

He held the boy close and forced the bile back down into his belly. Despite the animal urge to crush the boy in his arms, the Master kept a stone face and rocked the body 'til it became human again, allowing the slave in his arms to believe that his guide was doing what many Tops do: to keep an emotionless expression rather than expose their satisfaction and betray the macho facade that so often masquerades the true identity. The boy's emotional parachute had safely deployed, and the Master hurriedly but politely escorted the man to the door of the dungeon, where his guest's clothes were neatly folded. In short order, the slave dressed, profusely thanked his Master for the evening and exited, the radiance all but leaving a vapor trail down the driveway as he crossed the street to his car.

'*Go on and git,*' the Master thought.

He returned to the dungeon and looked at the scattered bits and pieces of the last 180 minutes. Stirrups hanging from the sling, a glove smeared and smelling of Vaseline lumped on the floor, various tools of the trade tossed like twigs in the corner. He knew he should clean his space before going to bed, but he didn't have the heart. Instead, he closed the door behind him and trudged out to the TV den, where he watched the news. When he finally did decide to go to sleep, he masturbated to the imagined thoughts of his guest's face, wrapped in duct tape, terrified and gag-pleading for help as his Master stuck his scrotum with fish hooks heated above a disposable lighter. The load was huge, far more satisfying than the one he had released earlier that evening.

Bottoms so often claim that their connection is an organic one, rooted in the spiritual center of the Earth. If so, he thought, do they realize that warmth is not always the molten gravity of the Earth's core, but could possibly be the fire just off the lip of a volcano? The thin skin of a blister waiting to explode out of the fragile crust? These slaves, so sure of their safety that they give permission to be made helpless and put into a circumstance shrouded only in trust; if they only knew, he thought. There's a certain appeal to danger and pain, oh yes. But if they knew the immediate danger they were flirting with and the pain he was feeling in the here and now. Afterglow, hell. He wanted the annihilation. He suspected sometimes the bottom on his torture table wanted it too…and he would sometimes seek those slaves out, the ones for which SM was little else than a transplanted death wish.

That was how it had been, for months now. His urge to wear his leathers had all but vanished, as had his reasons to attend events with his friends. His sessions, even with his regular fuck buddies, had become infrequent and unsatisfying, and he discovered that a beer and a good book were becoming far more interesting than KY and porno mags. He had even canceled some of his regular sessions, because he decided that the night's TV movie looked like something he could be interested in.

He knew something else, too. Fear. Fear that his fantasy life was becoming far more violent and he would envision himself taking these men from partner to prisoner or visitor to victim, and breaking the agreed upon limits. He even saw men on the street that he imagined pleading for their lives as he tied ropes to their wrists and ankles, men who he wouldn't have given a second glance to just a year ago. Seeing men, for whom SM was something CNN covered on weeks when a sensationalist headline was needed to cover a lame night of news, thrashing insanely as tight straps kept them from escaping the tightening ball crusher.

Why was he traveling off like this? He still looked good for a man in his 40's. His shirts still fit tightly to the creases of his body, and even if his face now creased when he smiled or squinted. A touch of grizzle beneath his moustache and shades kept a steady stream of newbies and experienced slaves inviting themselves to provide him with service. His reputation was always a gentleman sadist, an honorable man. But shit...he had to admit it, he was bored by the crowds of men he had seen continually for almost 20 years, bored by the fact that these same men still used public gatherings for little else than an excuse to act like irresponsible children and self-indulgent asses. Lately he hated these events and the people enough to avoid them altogether, from the fear of wanting to cause damage. Enough so to want to hang up his leathers for good, before he really did boil over. Enough so to recognize that he was barely a gentleman anymore, just tired. Tired and very, very bitter... and sad.

Scared that he had wasted all his time and effort on pushing an agenda that had no target, only a present. Bitter that the men he thought were friends were still running around idealizing the days "when" and often acting the part. Sad that the men that were really his friends had passed on to the next life, leading him to fend off a whole new generation of young men for whom loss was something laughed off as the reconstructed fables of old men with bad stories they wouldn't stop repeating. Men for whom the sky had fallen... and nothing had happened.

Boys for whom a leather bar was this month's experiment, expensive weekend costume fantasies their college loans allowed them to indulge in, only to be discarded like last week's next big thing. A place to play act on the internet between term papers and music video downloads. The most important right now until the computer was shut down or the beer money ran out... or parents called screaming about maxed-out credit cards.

He allowed himself a smile, and he felt those crows' feet even as he did. Here today, gone later today, he thought.

It's not that he didn't believe in God any more. It's just that lately God didn't seem to believe in him all that much. What if, then, a man decides to steal from God? The past, the Master mused, is imperfect and we are all imperfect people, the culture we live in thrives on that. It's one of the reasons we keep trying to reinvent ourselves and each other. We constantly try to label ourselves as Tops and bottoms, Masters and slaves, Daddies and boys. So often, we err; so often, we forget that the only way to invent the future is not to sit around talking about it.

The next day he wondered, "Do you remember the ones you don't love?" To create that kind of relationship, a love at last sight. It's kind of like wondering if you always have to settle for Mr. Right-Now. Right, now, right now. Everything is "right now." Everything is priority, nothing is prioritized... nothing can be finished in any order because it is part of an all-encompassing importunateness. Which then, the Master asked himself, is the most important "right now?"

The "right now" he did know was that he had made a commitment to the evening, a single tail demo for the pansexual group meet that night. This was the end, he told himself... after this night, a vacation from fetish world. The boy they offer may be hot, but I just can't face another group of probing brain-pickers.

Let them learn the way I did! Practice! Practice! Practice! He recalled the days he hadn't ever spoken of, when he would set pop cans on a wood fence and flick his first whip at them. It took months, but he became a flawless target thrower. Then and only then did he tie his first victim to a wooden cross and nick slowly at his shoulder blades. Whipping, crack by crack, till the tiny pinprick welts the Master stuck those muscles with had that first boy screaming, swaying, and suddenly gasping as the floodgates opened into his mind.

The Master remembered the beatific payload he dropped from his own loins as he saw the boy cross over, how he had to fight back the tears as he lowered the boy from the cross and heard the heart-rending hoarse whispering of "Thank you, Sir," repeated from the boy's lips over and over, seeing the glow of the boy's skin even in the dimmest light of the dungeon. But that was long ago. Payloads now felt more like ballast, lost at sea.

Tonight was not a challenge to share; it was a chore. Like all chores, he planned to endure it and finish the job, answer the perfunctory questions and get home in time for Conan. He dressed for the session and packed the best of his three whips, including that first one, gamy and frayed as it was. Just for nostalgia, he told himself. Again the smile... his second of the evening. He felt for a moment like he was tucking a rabbit's foot in the duffel for luck.

The group's clubhouse was a private warehouse in the loft district, high end enough to have a private parking garage, but still surrounded by burning drums of trash by the skid row seekers of heat and liquor. Once, as he pulled in for a different evening's demo, he recalled thinking that both the tribes of men inside this radius lived lives of outsiders... the men and women inside cloaking their world behind walls and hoods; the street people invisible by the plain-sighted existence of something to be feared by the population that pretended that none of this existed. Humans didn't beg for sustenance, and they certainly didn't beg to be tortured for sexual fulfillment.

Tonight he wondered if the muscular Master of Ceremonies ever even pondered what begging for mercy, real mercy, mercy from the people at large or mercy in the eyes of God could possibly feel like. He drove those thoughts from his mind and launched himself into his work of the evening. The boy was beautiful; someone had chosen well. His muscles were lightly developed, fair across his shoulders. His blindfolded face was framed from behind with a full head of hair, shaved up to the nape of his neck, leaving the full back open to a Master's strokes. Despite his ennui, a warmth trickled into his arms, the instinct of pleasure. If to go out, he thought, to go out on the blood of the beautiful. He massaged the boy's back and whispered calming, relaxing mantras to him, while explaining the importance of the safety and sanity of any scene to his audience. Words he knew by heart, had practiced for years, and wondered why anyone would need to hear them again and again...or was it (as he had begun to suspect) preamble to a voyeuristic peep show he was about to drive the boy with the beautiful back into.

'*Fuck all that,*' the Master kept thinking, '*he's too beautiful to wash in negative energy.*' The boy had relaxed in the warmth of the stage lighting and the Master's voice, at once directed to him and, in same time frame, some strange language to other people he was losing a karmic connection with, and the Master felt it, too. The time to lecture was done. The time to prove was right now. He ran his fingers through the bound man's hair, rubbing warmth into the shoulders of the man on the cross. He whispered to the bottom, "Now is yours," and stepped back to let his first throws breeze over the slave's back, then again across the ass. Not to touch, just to move air. To see those fair muscles clench in the manner their Creator intended. The design, the Master thought...the liquid of pride. The first touch, the oxygen sucked out from the room, the shrinking space between a Master and a subject, the tiny first welt. The fading away of the watchers, the disappearing walls, the moans of manhood rituals springing to life.

Needs are met, the Master thought. The call and response is answered in a circle of two. Each throw began to deliver what the Master remembered through the years, and the boy knew by his submissive instinct. Primal fear, bloodlust, alpha codes of males. Even in this mixed crowd, they bonded, the boy's moan's turning to gasps and then screams, the Master's arm extending the length of his lash. He abandoned, on that instinct, the whip he was using for his frayed "baby" of old and felt a sudden tingle of youth. Ageless courage beyond the months of disgust surging electrically as the whip melded into the glide of his whipping arm, a perfect rhythm to the man on the cross as his skin began to light up from heat. The Master could feel it, the tightness of the motions, the air that swam about his space and the slave's.

The golden glow off the skin of the boy, the Master imagined like an opening mountain. He knew what was coming, the boy was screaming, shuddering, the bound legs shaking, the vision blurring. The Master's vision. The Master's hearing. The Master knowing that a treasure was beholden to him right then, and he could feel it exploding deep inside of both of them, room full of onlookers be damned. The sharing of the vision struck him as their space went gold, expanding with light, and the mutuality of an Epiphany. For the first time in ages, the Master did something he hadn't permitted of himself. His spontaneous orgasm matched the cross-crushing pelvic thrusts of the slave. The cross quivered for that heavenly moment, and they shared the extraordinary joy. Both men could feel it, and the Master dropped his favorite tool and moved in quickly to the boy, kissing him gently on the neck, feeling the boy's warmth and hearing him gasp sweetly in bliss.

The Master could hear it in himself as well, just behind his ears. The bubbling pop pop pop of an air gun, he felt the same little twitches like kite cord going up his neck. His world, his heaven, opened wider before him as he took the boy's quivering body down from the cross, and was surprised when the boy, from a state where most men only quiver and quake, smiled blissfully and asked him, "What is it that you seek?"

"Redemption," the Master answered back. "To know before what I used to know." He stroked the markings on the boy, looking in awe at the golden seams his oldest and most trusted whip had left. As he touched the marks, they seemed to send out rays that held the Master's hand in gloved fists of purity.

"Follow," said the boy. "You can still see it. You never forget it."

The Master looked up at the corridors of the clubhouse that had gone invisible before, but the faces had changed. There was understanding, empathy there now, not the greedy dreams of the sexually insatiable. The Master could still feel those faces watching him as they changed to his old friends, the ones who's full lifetime of raptures had eluded him in their struggles and exits, and he realized what was happening. The calm in the oblivion had come to him there, as unelusive as all final destinies are. This right now was the most important right now of all, the moment of understanding. His friends reached out to him as the slave's whiplashes opened to show the gold of their wings, spreading beyond the dance of blindness and to the final steps that the angel led him. The hands of his friends took and lifted the Master's arms as he melted into the joy of infinity, and the Master heard the boy lilting as he floated down to earth below.

"There isn't any most important right now. It is only with every dream you allow yourself to envision, that you know what eternity can truly become."

By the guiding arms of the most important moments of his life, the Master felt the black wings of leather lead him to see the great spirits' faces at last.

CODE NAME: SWUFFY

Eight hours ago…

His eyes formed blurred vision. White bubbles swirled in his brain, as he slowly regained sense. He tried to remember when it happened before he lost consciousness. But for the moment, only fog appeared in his eyes. Awareness began to creep into his body. The white bubbles began to clear in his sight, and he felt tightness around his limbs, chest, and neck. There was a taste in his mouth that felt thick and dirty. An attempt to move his arms and legs led him to realize that he was strapped a chair, and the taste in his mouth was a leather plug somehow strapped around his head.

The sound of rattling chains made his vision completely clear. He was in some sort of brick or mud mortar structure, with open windows that had no glass and looked out over the desert. Directly in front of him were two gallows-like poles. His fellow soldiers Marcus and Bryson were hanging by their wrists. Halfway down each pole was a wooden adjunct that rested against their midsection. Their feet were spread apart by a pole that had restraints at each end, forcing their ankles apart. Those poles were fastened to the floor, securing the soldiers in a standing position. Their heads were covered with sacks, a band of cloth tied tightly across where their mouths would be in order to gag them.

With awareness came pain. He felt an intense throbbing in the side of his face. That's when he remembered the raid on their encampment. He was reaching for the keyboard of the top-secret computer that his unit was entrusted with, only to see the butt of a rifle coming towards his head. He now understood that he had been captured and was a prisoner of war. A sharp throb caused him to groan from the pain in his body. He heard a sound off to his side. Turning to look, he saw three men leaning intently over the laptop. One of them was sharply dressed in what seemed to be an almost formal camouflage uniform, while the other two just seemed like grunts. Instantly he realized who was in control. His stirrings had caught their attentions.

"Welcome to my camp," the commander announced. His skin was dark and he had a full jet-black mustache that covered his lip. Unlike the scruffiness of his two underlings, he was otherwise clean-shaven and had a presence. "I am Hushan," he informed his captive. "As you probably figured out, you and your two friends are the only survivors from your outpost. We also knew that your computer has a new communications and coordination system. We also know that, without the correct password, the hard drive will wipe itself clean if we enter incorrectly more than three times."

Hushan reached up and jerked the sacks from the heads of Bryson and Marcus. "Before this evening is through, one of you will give me the correct password." Bryson and Marcus were trying to shake the clouds from their eyes and adjust to the light. Marcus was spitting out the dirt and lint that the gag had forced into his mouth. Walking between them, Hushan stared at the prisoner he had strapped tightly into the hard chair. "Your two friends will go first." There was a sudden rush of noise as Bryson and Marcus struggled against their chains. "Who do you think is the weaker willed?"

The man in the chair could only stare at his oppressor. For some reason, Hushan had chosen not to unbuckle the leather gag that filled his mouth, while Marcus and Bryson's had been torn away. He could only follow the movements of Hushan and his two soldiers. Hushan pulled a long box over by the two gallows poles.

"Heat," he began, "is an amazing loosener of tongues. Some men, you give them whiskey and the warmth will soon have them talking like they've known you all your life. But we have no such comforts here." From an open hole in the top of the box, Hushan pulled out a length of wiry cord. It was rough looking, silver, and had orange bands marking distance and length. It seemed to be the thickness of a dime, and bent into shapes as Hushan coiled it around his arm. "This is a wonderful invention the Chinese gave us. It's a slow-burning fuse that they developed for mining. Eventually, they used it for fireworks."

His head slowly moved back and forth, staring between Marcus and Bryson. "A paper match burns at approximately 451°. A wooden match burns at 1000° – 1400°. A sparkler burns at 1,800°F – 3,000°F. Now imagine a very thick sparkler that burns very, very slowly. The inventors of these fuses calculated that they would burn a minute for each meter used." He stepped over to Bryson and began to wrap the fuse around his leg, up and around his chest, and counted the fifth orange marker before using a wire cutter to cut the fuse and tuck the tail end behind Bryson's ear. Marcus and Bryson began gasping for air, understanding what Hushan was planning.

"A fuse alone doesn't do it," explained Hushan with a sardonic authority. He reached into his shirt pocket and produced a white button-appearing object with two small wires extending from it. "To set off the explosion in the mine, you need one of these. A blasting cap." Hushan took the two small wires at the end of the cap and twisted them into the tail of the fuse. One of his soldiers handed him a small piece of duct tape, and Hushan secured the cap just behind Bryson's ear. "Normally, there are explosives with the blasting cap, but this close, we don't need it."

Hushan stared at the captive soldier in the chair, while reaching into another shirt pocket for a long cigar. He picked up a box of wooden matches, struck one, and puffed the cigar to life. "That's 5 meters," he declared. "5 minutes. It doesn't sound like much but when the flames start to crawl across your chest, you'll think it's five years." He turned to Bryson, and exaggeratingly opened and closed the wire cutter in front of his face. "All you have to do is tell me the password, and I will cut the fuse where it's burning. It will all stop."

He lowered the lit cigar to the end of the fuse sticking out from Bryson's leg. It sputtered, then burst into a sparking hiss of white flames, creeping towards Bryson's pants leg.

48 weeks earlier...

The commander had written the diagram across the chalkboard. "Gentlemen," he said sternly, "you have been brought here as the best of the best. What we want from you is a computer program that will coordinate field actions among a small network of no more than five computers in the field. This subset of computers will be able to bring battle factions together at a location point determined by the computer that initiates the sequence."

The men in the room slowly shared looks between each other. The encryption to do a small program like this and to share it was something that had only been talked about before. No one had ever done it. Much less taken it to a small-scale and on the battlefield itself. The commander continued, "The most important thing about this new program is that it absolutely cannot be cracked. Even if it means giving up your life to stop it."

Now the looks among the men in the room were more intense and far more confused. While fault tolerance and secrecy were already a high priority, no one had ever discussed a program as being worth a soldier's life. The commander continued to outline the specifications of what he wanted this program to do. "Should any one of the five computers be activated," he said, "before other battalions should be able to locate the initial signal, rendezvous there within 30 minutes, and proceed to engage the enemy. The most important aspect of this network is that all of the computers and IT be completely and intimately aware of the surrounding routes and potential hazards that would lead to the rendezvous points. Each battalion should be able to use its computer to rendezvous in a sequenced and coordinated manner with the first battalion to move and the initial battalion to send out the signal." He pounded his fist on the chalkboard for emphasis. "If this works, it will be the most effective attack coordinator that we have ever known in our armed forces. I need this in less than a year."

Swofford exchanged a glance with Hoffman. Then they both turned to Miller. They both knew that if anyone could figure out this complex encryption, Miller was the man. As the commander left the room, Swofford and Hoffman immediately got up and stood at opposite sides of Miller's chair. Swofford made the first move. "You want to be on our team?" he asked. A smile slowly cracked across Miller's face. "I was wondering if the Army would ever give me a challenge."

Seven-and-a-half hours later...

From his chair, the bound man watched as the flame moved the short length of the fuse to Hoffman's pants leg. A sudden burst of acrid odor struck his nose as the flame scorched the camouflage. The chains around Hoffman's wrists clanked loudly at the moment the flame first touched skin. Hoffman tried in vain not to cry out, but the slow-moving white arcs were soon too much for him. The bound man realized that he wasn't hearing the scream, but an anguished howl as the fuse burned its way.

Hushan stood before Hoffman silently, slowly opening and closing the wire cutters before his face. Not that it seemed to matter; as Hoffman violently writhed, the bound man along with Bryson watched the slow crawl of the flame from Hoffman's waist to his lower chest. "Swuffy! Swuffy! Swuffy, don't tell them." He shook and shouted in the only moment of his torture that he did not scream, "Don't tell them Swuffy," The flame rose to the center of his chest, and the screens and howls resumed.

With an abrupt turn towards the bound man, Hushan moved towards the chair. "Swuffy?" He asked. "That's the code word?" He grabbed the gag across the bound man's lips and tore it away violently. The leather snaps and strap cracked as the bound man's face rocked forward.

The bound man spit, bits of leather and saliva flying toward Hushan. "No you asshole, that's my name." Hushan stared, eyes narrowed. "My name is Swofford. First they called me Swoffy, then someone called me Swuffy. It's what everyone in my unit calls me."

Hushan spit on the floor and cursed, as Hoffman's screams began to turn into voiceless cries, Hushan shoved his face into Swofford's. "Swuffy," he sneered derisively. "What kind of nickname is that? My nickname. They call me Urso. The bear. I can rip your chest apart with my hands." He pointed towards one of his accomplices who was still standing by the laptop. "He is scorpion. His sting can kill. Swuffy." Again, Hushan spat on the floor and cursed. "Your nickname sounds like a child's toy. Like something you would find in a baby's bed. You Americans. Soft. Just like your nicknames."

By now, the fuse on Hoffman's body had reached his neck. He had torn his vocal cords apart from the pain. Hushan stepped behind Swofford's chair and grasped Swofford's head between his two strong hands. He twisted Swofford's neck until he could not help looking directly at Hoffman. Swofford could see the flame slowly duck behind Hoffman's ear. "Well, Swuffy," Hushan ordered, "Watch your friend die."

Swofford closed his eyes as tightly as he could, but that did not block out the loud crack of the blasting cap. Nor did it stop the splatter that struck his face. A syrupy goo spattered against his forehead and cheeks, and he could feel the gel as it began to ooze down. He couldn't bear to open his eyes.

14 weeks earlier...

Miller was exasperated. He and Swofford had already figured out how to coordinate a network of computers to align command positions and attack positions. What they hadn't yet figured out was how to encode messages traveling between the network to make them less likely to be intercepted and decoded by an enemy combatant. Swofford and Miller had suggested to Hoffman that they try to find to multiple encapsulations for messages to make it harder to get inside the encryption.

Hoffman argued that, for the most part, double encapsulations have pretty much been figured out by everyone. If any low-level hacker could, Miller also noted that there were rumors that the Chinese had already worked up to a triple relation. Somehow, they had to find a way to make the encapsulation coded along with the encrypted message inside. Should any one of the computers be captured and the program be compromised, it would put all the computers in the network at risk to be discovered for their locations.

Hoffman was ready to call it a night. He scrawled a few more notes on the board to save for the following day before packing his briefcase and heading off for his cabin. Swofford smiled and turned his glance towards Miller. They had fairly little time alone, and fell into a passionate embrace. Knowing that Hoffman had gone, they locked the door to the lab and carefully begin removing each other's clothing.

"At last," sighed Miller, "this work is draining me." He let his tongue dance along Swofford's neck before embracing him in a full kiss. "I feel like a dirty schoolboy."

Swofford couldn't help but giggle. The only thing appropriately placed was an old couch along the side of the room. But with that being the only option, they took advantage. Swofford gripped the arm of the couch as Miller slid inside of him. They rocked back and forth slowly, knowing that this rare moment of privacy might not come again soon. They could feel each other against their skins, allowing the sweat to slide between them. Swofford clutched the sofa as he felt Miller tensing up to a climax. There was a muffled yell as Miller let loose.

"Sometimes I hate being an open secret," Miller sighed as he rolled off Swofford's back. Swofford could not help but laugh again. "All for the sake of national security," he said with a chuckle. He reached over and began to peel off Miller's condom. Within a moment, inspiration struck him.

He held the spent condom in his hand and stared at it. "Miller, we're doing this backwards." When Miller looked at Swofford puzzlingly, Swofford continued. "It's not the message we should be encapsulating and encoding, the message should be the encapsulation." He jumped to the blackboard and quickly began writing algorithms beneath the notes that Hoffman left. "What if we designed the code that surrounded the intended message, but was the message itself, and could be infinitely encapsulated?"

Miller's eyes went wide. "My God," he said in a hushed voice. "Could it really be that simple?"

6 hours later…

Hushan's minions had pulled the bloody body of Hoffman from his chains, and were dragging it from the room when Hushan stopped them. There was a crater in the back of Hoffman's head, and a flap of skin blown forward by the blasting cap. Hushan stopped his men and plucked a hunting knife from his camos. He grabbed the flap of skin, glowering at Swofford, and sliced it off. Motioning his minions to continue, he waved the skin in Swofford's face. Swofford realized that Hushan had cut off Hoffman's ear.

"So Swuffy," he leered, "is this the business you wanted to be in?" He turned towards Bryson, who had been silently pulling against his restraints. "How long do you think you'll last?" Hushan tucked the ear into a pouch attached to his belt.

"About as long as it took me to fuck your mother," Bryson retorted.

Without missing a beat, Hushan spun on his heel and drove both his fists, clenched together, into Bryson's solar plexus. Even chained with his hands over his head, Bryson doubled over as far as he could from the punch. As he tried to straighten out, Hushan drove his balled up fists into Bryson's gut a second time. This time, the blow caused Bryson to vomit.

Scorpion and the other lackey had already come back in from disposing of Hoffman's body outside the building. Hushan flicked his head towards the pool on the floor, and the two men immediately began toweling it off. "Americans," snorted Hushan. "You think everything is like a movie. 'Diehard'. 'Top Gun'. Everything a quick comment or smart remark."

"I'm not going to beg," gasped Bryson.

There was a bark of laughter as Hushan began pulling fresh fuse from the box of cord. "Oh, you'll beg. They all beg." He measured five orange marks before snapping the wire cutters on the cord. "Your friend," he chuckled at Bryson, "he had more bravery than you'll ever know. When he finally begged, he didn't scream to his God or cry to his mama, he called for his commanding officer to be brave. Do you think you can be that brave?"

This time, Bryson stayed silent. Hushan stared him down. When Bryson finally broke eye contact, Hushan laughed again. "Just as I thought," he said, "sometimes you know when to keep your mouth shut." He placed the cord on the table next to his cigar ashtray, and reached into his pocket. He took a box cutter and extended the razor next to Bryson's cheek. "Your friend lasted through all 5 meters without telling me what I need, and with his clothes on." He took the box cutter and sliced it down the length of Bryson's tank top. "How do you think the burning will feel directly on your skin?" Hushan tossed the shredded shirt aside and began sawing through Bryson's braided belt.

As the belt frayed in half, Hushan sliced down both pants legs and pulled Bryson's legs bare. Hushan stood back admirably gazing at Bryson's body. Bryson took a lot of pride in his physique, and worked hard to keep his body chiseled. "What a soldier you are," Hushan mocked. He took his hand and reached under Bryson's boxer shorts. There was a hiss of breath as Bryson felt Hushan jerk his cock and balls out from under the shorts. "Your pride will burn nicely."

Taking the end of the cord, Hushan wrapped a tight loop around Bryson's testicles. He did a small spin of the cord once around Bryson's penis before pulling the cord up the crack of the boxer shorts and wrapping it around Bryson's stomach.

Continuing to taunt Bryson, Hushan made a special effort to pull the fuse tightly across Bryson's chest, taking care to make sure that each nipple would feel the sear of the fuse's burning flames. Hushan wrapped the final piece of cord around Bryson's neck. "You bastard," Bryson hissed.

"Again, you really should learn to keep your mouth shut," Hushan taunted. He finished into his front pocket for another blasting cap and from the table pulled a long strip of duct tape. He fastened the blasting cap at the back of Bryson's chin, well wrapping the tape around Bryson's head, sticking the tape into Bryson's flattop. "This time, I think we'll just take it off for good."

Hushan retrieved his cigar from the ashtray, struck a match, and puffed it back to life. To further torment Bryson, he kept blowing large clouds of smoke directly into his face. Bryson knew full well that Hushan was trying to mind fuck him, to goad him into more verbal sparring. Hushan eventually tired of this and touched the burning end of the cigar to the end of the fuse. "Kiss your family jewels goodbye," he said, and jammed the lit cigar into Bryson's waist. The fuse sputtered and began to creep towards Bryson's foreskin.

Bryson managed not to scream when the lit cigar crushed against his skin. But he could feel his scrotum desperately trying to retract in fear, and the tight loop of fuse holding his testicles in a trap. He stared defiantly at Hushan, who stood in front of him, arms crossed with a scoffing smile on his lips. His determination to fight the torture only lasted as long as it took for the first sparks to singe his most intimate area.

Swofford could hardly help himself, or keep himself from staring as his fellow soldier was meeting with the cruelest of pains. Bryson's bellow was mighty as Swofford watched the flame slowly circle Bryson's penis and crawl from the shaft to the bound balls. He could feel his stomach wrenching, watching

Hushan waving the wire cutters in front of Bryson, as Bryson screamed obliviously. When the fuse reached Bryson's ball sack, the screams turned to high-pitched wails, keening and echoing against the building's walls.

"Say it," whispered Hushan, "say it."

The fuse continued to burn, and Swofford could smell the terrible stench of burning flesh and hair, as the fuse mercifully completed its horrific orbit and began creeping back into Bryson's shorts. Bryson again began to heave, but he had already spilled his guts from the earlier punches. He screamed again, rapidly shaking his head from side to side, and fainted.

Hushan quickly stepped in, and snipped the fuse where it was burning behind Bryson's back. "Pussy," he cursed under his breath. "You don't get to sleep your way through this."

13 weeks earlier...

Miller and Swofford looked at their newly-configured encryption codes. When they'd explained it to the brass the week before, they ditched the condom allusion and switched to a chain mail idea, where the protective suit of links had the message interwoven as many times as you needed it, while the body inside was essentially a dummy message. You could plant whatever you wanted to inside, but that wasn't the pure information. Swofford sent the field commander a message that appeared to give a set of coordinates three miles away, then asked him to use the new program to decode it.

The face on the conference call blanched. "Turn your screen to the camera," Swofford jibed him. The room broke into laughter as a photoshopped picture of the FC appeared in a bikini, holding an M-16. As the laughter died down, Swofford addressed the gathered. "We can send any number of messages this way, while the decoders think they're reading something else. We can also tell who is reading the wrong messages if we think the system is compromised." When asked how, Swofford held up a little blue circuit. "Double blind tracking," he smiled.

5 hours later...

Hushan wiped his hands across the crisp creases of camouflage. Scorpion and the other minion had wiped away the area in front of Bryson and stood ready each with a bucket full of water. The smoke from Hushan's cigar drifted through the shafts of light in their makeshift torture chamber.

Swofford watched helplessly as Hushan cocked his head towards the two assistants, who hauled back and emptied their buckets forcefully into Bryson's face. Bryson sputtered and screamed as the pain returned to his body. "Even your companion could stay conscious during his torture," Hushan said with contempt. "You barely made it halfway."

Tears were streaming down Bryson's face. Swofford had never seen his tough fellow soldier break apart like he was now. Hushan had bent the fuse back towards the front of Bryson's body, where Bryson could see it. He purposely puffed the cigar smoke directly into Bryson's eyes, before slowly and theatrically lowering the glowing tip to the end of the fuse. Even with the water dripping off his body, the fuse against Bryson's skin crackled back into flame. The sparkling white burning resumed its cruel track along Bryson's chest. In a frightening turn, Bryson began to cry, in violent sobs, wailing at the top of his lungs.

"Mother! Mother!"

Swofford could see a grin playing across Hushan's face. He began to wonder if Hushan's goal was to even get the password from Bryson, or if burning Bryson's flesh and blowing his jaw off was more important to the terrorist. Was he secretly getting a thrill out of the pain he was inflicting on the muscular American soldier? Bryson's cries of pain could no longer articulate any words, just agony as the slow-moving flames crossed his chest, burning each nipple and creeping towards his neck.

Hushan turned to Swofford, the smile now evilly evident. "Your friend," he said devilishly, "made himself strongly on the outside, but inside, he is weak. Tell me, Swuffy, which one are you? Do you have the courage of your first soldier, or the distasteful weakness of the friend here?" The fuse had little length left to it, and Swofford could see the tiny amount of space before the blasting cap under Bryson's chin. This time Swofford couldn't turn away, and the crack blew Bryson's skull backwards, while ripping the jawbone from his face and sending it flying across the floor.

"Your friend," gestured Hushan towards Bryson, "was a fool. No matter how strong he thought he was, no matter how many sit-ups, push-ups, or weightlifting he thought could save him, they all die. They all bleed. And they all cry, begging." With another flick of his head, Hushan's two helpers began the horrific task of taking Bryson down from the scaffold. "Tell me again, Swuffy, when the flames are kissing your flesh, how much do you think you can take?"

6 weeks earlier...

The test models of the five computers had worked exactly as Hoffman, Miller and Swofford had planned. The field exercises both locally, and in diverse locations, had performed exactly as specified. Artificial intelligence that Swofford had programmed had also performed to expectations. Utilizing a GPS function similar to tracking cell phones enabled the computers to be monitored for location, movement, and distance.

But most importantly, the new encoding sequences seemed virtually foolproof. Swofford's superiors repeatedly praised his innovative work, commenting that he may have just invented a new military technology that could change the face of field maneuvers. Swofford always gave Miller and Hoffman the credit he felt they equally deserved. But secretly, they both knew that it was Swofford's ideas that had made the system possible.

The decision was made to take the five prototypes into the theater. Swofford, Miller, and Hoffman were informed that they would each accompany a computer as an embedded technician. There was some objection to Swofford's participation, and that he was the architect of the system and putting him in harm's way might be too great of a risk. It was Swofford himself who made the final call. "It will only be for eight weeks," he reasoned, "and I would like to be available if the system functions improperly at any point."

That night, Miller clutched Swofford in his arms, sobbing softly. "This is the most dangerous area of the war," he protested. "I don't like being separated from you, especially under those kinds of conditions." It had been determined that while Hoffman and Swofford would be deployed to the same unit, Miller would be sent to one of the other four units. Three other technicians that worked on the project would be deployed with the other three computers. But it was Swofford that Miller feared for.

Waist to waist, they caressed each other knowing that in two more weeks, they would be separated in the desert mountains. Miller pressed himself into Swofford's lips, his kisses almost desperate. As they made love, Swofford returned his kiss, understanding his lover's concern, and feeling a tiny twinge of fear. His confidence was not often to be shaken, that both he and the love of his life would soon be under combat made him tingle with nervousness. While he knew that his fellow soldiers were some of the most specially trained in the entire military and that he and his fellow technicians would be regarded as high-value associates, this was both his partner and his program design. Those twinges were going to remain a tingle that he would not be able to shake up to the day of their deployment.

4 hours later...

The grisly remains of Bryson had been dragged outside, laid with Hoffman's to rot in the desert sun. Hushan was completely aware that Swofford knew that this was meant as the highest form of insult. The maimed bodies of his comrades were exposed to the vultures and dogs. Hushan and his minions did it both as humiliation and as a message to Swofford. The cigar that Hushan had used to ignite the fuse that ultimately took the lives of the two soldiers had been crushed out into the ashtray.   Pacing in front of Swofford, Hushan continued playing his dangerous psychological game of cat and mouse. All Swofford could think about was the site of the flying jawbone as it ripped away from Bryson's skull, and the site of Hushan, in his sharply defined camouflage uniform taking the ears of the soldiers for his trophy bag. The computer still sat on the table, just feet away from where Swofford sat, helplessly confined.

He remembered the explicit order at the beginning of the mission. That this program was of the highest importance, even if it meant giving up one's life. He'd already seen two brave men sacrifice themselves in order to keep that secret. But now he knew that he would be the last line of defense between the enemy and what they considered a highly valuable target.

Hushan was happy to see Swofford's mental anguish. He continued his silent pacing, knowing that the longer his prisoner tried to process the situation, the greater advantage the he would have. However, he had one more bit of unused information to ply Swofford into his court. He kicked the leg chair, hard enough to recapture Swofford's attention. "You realize that I cannot kill you," Hushan said, in his gentlest voice. "I know that you are the architect. Your two friends, just collateral. I could play with them, like mice. I could show you cruel depravity, and kill them without loss."

A cold realization began to form in the pit of Swofford's stomach. Hushan knew? How much? And how? How did he find out? Swofford, even more than when he was forced to watch the torture of his companions, felt a sickness begin to form inside. Somehow, someone had been leaking information to the enemy. Even in the secret laboratories where he and Miller had developed their program, there had been a spy.

And somehow, that spy had delivered him to Hushan and his sadistic henchmen. He felt the blood drain from his face.

"Don't look so surprised," Hushan continued, in a voice both gentle and patronizing. "We have men everywhere, and women. You could not be corrupted, but there are plenty around you that could be. So while your friends were disposable, you are not. You are a commodity. You can be traded. Whether I trade you for men or for information, I don't know. I do know that I cannot kill you." The sneering grin returned. "But I can still hurt you. And it is only the torturer who enjoys the torture."

Another cock of his head brought Scorpion and the other lackey to the contraption that had been holding Swofford for the past several hours. They began to undo the bindings that had been holding him fast. "I have two directives," Hushan began, "you're to give me the password to this computer, and then I am to deliver you and you will create the same program under our supervision. If you don't," he paused to chuckle, bending at the knees so he was face-to-face with Swofford, "you'll wish that I'd used blasting caps on you."

Unrestrained from the chair, Hushan's minions pulled the chains from one of the around Swofford's wrists. His legs were forced apart and cuffed to the separation bar. He was soon as helpless as Bryson and Hoffman had been. Swofford watched in horror as Hushan pulled one meter of cord from his box and coiled it in and around his thigh. Hushan took a fresh cigar from the front pocket of his camouflage, struck a wooden match until the cigar was fully burning. "Are you as strong as your friend? Or as weak as the other?" He blew smoke across the tip of the cigar, watching as the flame flashed. "You know what I want. Now tell me how much you value your pride. I might not be able to blow it off; but burning it off, you can live without it." Hushan held the cigar close to Swofford's face and locked eyes with his captive. He followed Swofford's gaze as the cigar began to lower down to the fuse coiled at his hip.

Swofford contained his fear, but he knew what he had to do. "I'll give you the password."

Five weeks earlier...

The field-testing had also been a place for Swofford and Miller to test the double blind. How, one of the commanders wanted to know, could we protect the computers if one fell to enemy hands? Swofford already had put into place the feature that would irreversibly corrupt the hard drive if a password had been entered more than five times incorrectly. But they also knew that just about everyone knew that security feature was standard. They needed some other way to protect the system. More to the point, they needed a way to track a captured computer without giving away the locations of the other four. Miller made an offhand comment about emergency intervention. Then Hoffman made a joke that it was supposed to be I before E except after C. Every dummy knew that. And the lightbulb went off in Miller's head.

One hour later...

Swofford thought he saw a look of disappointment cross Hushan's face when he pulled the cigar back from the fuse without getting to light it. His brow furrowed, Swofford was unsure if it was from anger or confusion. Still, Hushan cocked his head and grumbled something to Scorpion. The two lackeys began to take away the restraints and chains that were supporting Swofford against the scaffold. When they had unbound him, they pushed him into a chair against the table where the computer had been sitting all this time.

"Okay Swuffy," scowled Hushan. "Show me what you're made of."

Swofford single finger pecked S-W-U-F-F-I-E at the keyboard in front of them. Hushan broke into a hearty genuine laugh. "So that was it all along. You let your friend die for nothing. Remember that when you're re-creating this program for me." The screen in front of them filled with topographic images of the surrounding landscape. Four red pinpoints arrayed themselves on the screen. A countdown clock appeared in the top left corner, a star formed on the screen, representing Swofford's computer location.

"What is that clock for?" Hushan asked. Swofford felt a metallic nudge against the side of his head. From the corner of his eye, he saw Scorpion pressing a pistol to the side of his skull. This would be the real test of all the work he, Miller and Hoffman had put into not only the computer program itself, but their security protections that they specially designed for this network.

The other four red pinpoints began to move. "That clock," Swofford explained, "represents the amount of time it will take the other four units to converge on this location. What I've just done is tell them that they should come here prepared for combat, but the system will coordinate their attack." The countdown clock had just passed 40 minutes. "The farthest unit is 40 minutes away and if you follow the markers, their trackers will show their motion towards me."

"Where I will wait for them," Hushan declared. He stared intently at the screen as the most distant red pinpoint merged with a second. "Those two units, they now head towards us?"

Swofford swallowed hard. "Yes."

Hushan grinned at his prisoner. He picked up a radio device and began speaking quickly into it. Swofford was unable to follow most of what he had said, but 40 minutes was repeated several times. It was easy to figure out that Hushan was calling for a strike against the other four units in motion. The clock in the corner ticked down to the 37-minute mark. The two moving pinpoints soon met with the third, and it joined in the motion towards Swofford's.

"Like the tiger that waits in the grass, my prey will come to me," Hushan stated as he put the radio down. "You serve me well, Swuffy. All we need to do is wait. You will see these dogs die as you did your friends." The clock on the screen turned to 35. There was silence as the pinpoints moved closer to Swofford's.

Swofford hoped that he had enough time. Hushan had called for reinforcements, and knew that they had to get there before the pinpoints converged on the computer screen. The minutes ticked as they watched in the heat. Swofford felt his stomach clench as the clock narrowed down to the 20-minute mark.

Hushan motioned for Scorpion to handcuff and gag Swofford. The clock on the computer ticked past the 30-minute marker while Swofford and Hushan stared at the red pinpoints headed towards their location. Ten more minutes, Swofford thought to himself. Just ten more minutes...

Scorpion had shifted to the open window of the room, with Hushan and the other minion nearby. They obviously were looking for the reinforcements that he'd called for when Swofford heard the first double swish of air and saw Scorpion and his partner hit the ground, both with clean headshots. There was a cry from Hushan, who aimed his pistol directly at Swofford as he spun away from the window, but it was already too late. Sniper bullets slammed into his arm and hip, knocking the gun across the floor and dropping Hushan to the ground.

Swofford looked at the computer, which had just passed the 24-minute mark. Not only were the troops in to rescue him, there were six minutes ahead of time. Hushan was trying to pull himself toward his pistol, but an American uniform leapt through the door and kicked the gun aside while also landing a boot into Hushan's ribcage. Swofford didn't even need to see his rescuer's face, just by his profile, he knew. It was Miller, come to save him from this living Hell.

30 days earlier...

When they were finally able to properly configure the redundancy into all the computers, Miller was the one to explain it to the brass. "Each computer will have dual passwords," he told them. "If one of the computers is in a tech's possession should the enemy capture him, he can enter the alternate password, but with the letters IE at the end and minus the final letter. That sends an alarm to the other four computers that the program has been compromised and set up a retrieval and rescue. The motion sensors will automatically send bogus location information and the reconnaissance clock will show twice the time instead of the actual ETA." The room breathed in a gasp of relief and recognition; not only could the program not be easily stolen, it could also be used to locate enemy strongholds if compromised.

26 minutes later...

Miller had already uncuffed and removed his lover's gag, and was holding him in a tight embrace. "It had to be me," he told Swofford. "I couldn't bear the thought of anyone else getting to you and risk that loss." Meanwhile, Hushan was chained up against the scaffolds he'd used to murder Bryson and Hoffman. The platoons had already reconned the bodies of the two dead soldiers, and were well aware that there were mere minutes before Hushan's troops would arrive expecting to ambush them.

But there was still enough time for one more thing. Swofford took three one-meter cords of fuse and wrapped one around Hushan's groin, one in circles around his neck, and the third into a gas can set between Hushan's legs. "They all beg, you told me," Swofford growled at his one-time captor. "Who will you beg in the last minute of your life?" He took the wooden matches off the table and lit each of the three fuses. "Which one will reach a blasting cap first? Your neck? Your cock? Or the tank of gasoline? Too bad we'll already be gone."

The soldiers outside honked the horns of their jeeps, signaling they were ready to get out, now. There was a deep groan as the first fuse licked at Hushan's skin. Swofford buried his tongue one more quick time in Miller's mouth as the two sprinted to the awaiting Jeep.

BLAINE

"Why all this constant grousing about being a man?" Blaine asked me. "Even a gay man has it better than most of the population in this country. For Christ's sake, you're all but born with a silver spoon between your legs and you're whining that no one will let you be who you want to be!"

The conversation had spun out of control quite a ways back, as they always seemed to when Blaine and I spoke. I had my own set of clichés that I despised; he had his. Yet he was the closest friend I had who could – or wanted to – follow my track when discussing more than sports and weather, or whose body was hotter in what movie in a given genre and year, or why Aerosmith was a better 70's dance band than The Commodores. Blaine was one of but a few voices in an ocean of conformity, and one of the few friends I could depend upon to not spend countless wasted words on gay-speak.

He'd even relayed it to me one morning after a rubber session when I finally asked him, "What is it you see in me?"

Blaine had to stop for a second. His key ceased jiggling in the padlock for a moment; his eyes moved away from the bedpost and to my still-hooded face. His big brown eyes narrowed to a squint as he pondered the question. I was sure he knew his answer as soon as I asked, but he would never allow himself the appearance of being able to spike me with too ready a reply. His answer started out slow, then picked up momentum when he was certain of his words. "In the morning after we wake up from a night of hard, satisfying leather-sex," he began, "I never have to be afraid of you not having something to say. I know that the first thing out of your mouth won't be some idiotic blather or worse yet, that you won't have anything at all to say. Sometimes I may accuse you of thinking too much, but I'll never accuse you of insufficient thinking. There have been many desperate evenings when I've woken up to a morning's worth of self-questioning about how this 'thing' got into my bed. Jim, I've gone to bed with more than my share of stupid men. But not you. You, bless you, are never stupid."

Of course I love him, and have for the past seventeen years. The ties between Blaine and me are more spiritual than anything else, our mutually conflicting schedules prevent our paths from crossing in any more than a few months each year.

Here I am then, again given the chance to stare into the most sexual eyes I've ever known and give in to the most thoroughly in-control man I've ever met. In the life that I have lived so far, I tally Blaine on the small finger-count of friends that truly matter, a man who is as much kinsman as Master. Yet even now we were engaged in the kind of argumentative exercise that he loves drawing me into. I've often felt that this was just as much a testing of my limits as anything he ever tried in a scene.

"Fuck being servile!" Blaine was roaring away at me over some off-the-cuff comment I'd made about slaving. "That's just pretending! Deep down inside, you want to be a Man with another Man. If someone isn't letting you be what you really want to be or what you really are, get the hell away from him, because he's just slumming for a blowjob. Only if your balls are in danger of exploding unless you con a trick into a night of horny sex, don't pretend for anybody!" He placed his head in his hands for a moment to catch his breath and gather his thoughts, then he looked up from his seat at me. "Jim, today we will take a special journey together. I know we've gone off on some ingenious pathways before, but this time we'll make some stops along the route. I think there are some things we should try to explain to each other."

I have to admit, what Blaine was trying to say at first eluded me. There had never been a session with him, from our initial meeting when he handcuffed me to a bed with a rubber sheet stretched out tight beneath me, to the last time we saw each other in a New York City hotel when our paths crossed while traveling, that hadn't been anything less than a dual epiphany. "I'm ready, Sir."

"Then strip."

These are the words that mark the beginning, the transition. Blaine gives me that first simple two-word command and our bond shifts from an equidistant orbit given of friendship to the teetering balance of an erotic fulcrum, a delicately shared geometric formula based on elaborate sexual equations. I shed my clothes directly and await my next order, already feeling those inner doors emerging from behind their barricades.

"The same rules as always, Jim, with one new directive. Answer all questions fully and without hesitation. Follow commands as you always have, with your usual obedience." Blaine removed his shirt and wrapped his arms around me, compressing me in his grip.

"Get on your knees and hold me," Blaine ordered. I did so without question. "Now tell me. Isn't this comfortable? Don't you feel like you belong here?"

"Yes Sir," I replied, my arms around his calves. "It feels like the only place I should be."

His hand stroked through my hair. "Do you feel like any less of a man because you're on your knees?"

"No Sir, not with you."

My head jerked back as Blaine pulled my hair down, forcing my face to stare up at his. "That's the whole point. Anytime you submit without surrender, you can't be a whole man, you're only playing a role. Stop trying to be Mister Best Boy and learn that for every time you give into a strong Master, the two of you are Men In Love for the duration of your scene because of the levels of your interactions. This is adult sexual contact. It is about spirit, not fakery; it is about who we are, not a costume or a play character. It's about my desire to let you just fucking uncork and submit, damn you. I don't want you on your knees with an 'A+ slave' attitude; I want you on your knees because you know you belong there and want to be there."

He backed away from me and I went into proper stance, eyes down, hands behind. Blaine returned with a rubber collar-to-wrist restraint, fastening it into place. "Stand."

With a fair amount of difficulty, I pulled myself to my knees, then balanced myself until I stood, legs splayed, before him. I heard the cold click of chain links when a support chain was attached from the ceiling to my collar. As the "ffsssss" of air squeezed from a pair of snakebite cups pressed against my nipples, he startled me by asking, "Why would you direct so much attention and affection to a man that for but two or three times a year, you don't even see?"

Through the first tantalizing wet tingles of suction, I replied, "Sir, if you wonder why this boy waxes enthusiasm in your direction, it's because he believes in the concept of extended families. It isn't the proximity of the man but his qualities. So even if we may be on the opposite sides of the continent, my fondness for you need not be constrained by my ability to see or be touched. My greatest fear in life is to actually end a relationship as close as I feel for you in the manner where the final line, 'He thinks of me as him,' is the epitaph of what you remember."

My nipples distended into their rubber confines as I continued. "There are too many exceptional people, of which YOU are one, who contribute to my life in such strongly positive ways that I work hard to not let that happen. Again, I think of you often and in warm manners. Whatever links of spirituality my body challenges me with, you are a link to my family here on Earth, and as such, one of the people I consider as a close kin – a brother, a Mentor, and friend."

Through the duration of my answer, Blaine was sliding a rubber ring over my cock and balls with a fireman's boot set at the end of a short tether. When he was finished, he gave it a bat and left the boot swaying between my legs. "You'll always have that, Jim," he answered. "Even if I care enough about you to want to see you getting more. Each of us needs to find kindred spirits in this world that we have dealt with ironically. Honesty is the rush. My friendships and contacts in these areas are limited deliberately so I can invest an appropriate amount of time in the 'right' friends. I manage to do well by those I care for. I want you to know clearly that for me, 'dominant' is a very rich facet of who I am. It is complete and very deeply part of me. I don't play games. I just am what I am. That's what makes the sex good and powerful.

"Most Tops don't know how to do what I am talking about. It takes a lot of experience and heart to learn, and honesty. But I find that few men are spiritually ready for the level of intensity and eroticism that I want and expect. This is the reason both why my stable is so small, less than you can count on one hand, and why you have been admitted. I knew early on, in my gut, seventeen years ago, you were ready for this and could understand it. It's why I reject cruelty and the vicious abuse that some Tops dish out. I'll admit, I can be sadistic, but it takes a hell of a bottom with a powerful spirit to bring it out in me. When it happens, the sadism always reconciles in a flood of emotion and protectiveness."

That was not a declaration I ever expected to hear anyone, including Blaine, convey during the course of a session. Even one as odd as this. "Protectiveness, Sir?"

"Jim, it's not about 'Top' and 'bottom' but shared power of soul in a very elegant and erotic exchange. A minuet of sorts. The power of both must be present or it doesn't work. Period."

"The music or the dance, Sir?"

"Probably both, Jim. I would more simply say that the whole encounter is ritual in nature, and the act of ritual is for both parties to 'cross over' into a sacred space where deeper elements of life may be expressed. A ritual by definition has an end, and the point is for you to realize inner levels of strength. I ask you, what is your definition of humiliating?"

A blindfold covered my eyes, taking away my visual connection to the scene, increasing my reliance on Blaine. Wherever he was leading me, I was now dependent on his descriptions of the immediate world to retain an understanding of its form. As meager a departure as it may seem, it forced me to pay stricter attention to the tonic of his voice as he continued to describe his thoughts. I drew a deep breath and answered, "to go through the motions when deeper feelings are present and could be touched and engaged?"

A slow caress of Blaine's fingers along my ribs raised gooseflesh and indicated that my answer pleased him. "Why do I often wear boots in a scene?" Blaine slapped the fireman's boot dangling between my legs and I groaned, for him. Continuing as the boot swung back and forth off my balls, "it symbolizes the Master, grounded by gravity, must remain in the real world of safe sex and protection and care for his charge." I could hear the rattle of a metal stand being wheeled next to me, then recognizing it as the holder of Blaine's suspended bright red water bladder. Its narrow hose was slipped into the boot off my crotch and I listened while Blaine clicked open the valve at the underside of the sack. A gradual trickling of fluid began to fill the boot, a slowly timed weight dragging my ball-sac towards the floor.

"You are correct in that what I speak of takes time, but the time is worth it. The fundamental issue is that I won't accept role playing because I am too experienced and too old for it. I want a man to be ready to submit, to be at my feet and be IN that state. I want him to feel owned, possessed, and ultimately free of ego/personality. I can GIVE you that, Jim. Why should I or you accept less?"

Grunting through this new pulling at my groin, I gasped, "I know why I accept less on many occasions. It's called loneliness. I've tried a couple of times to break off relationships when they feel forced. Yet there's a very basic part of my psyche that pushes everything out of the way at times. That's why, when a Master calls, my submissiveness overwhelms my rationale and I go. The part of me that desires and needs the bondage and S/M just can't be denied. Surrendering to you, Sir, is always easy enough, because I already have great respect for your ideas and for you as an intellect."

The time and gravity comments were not lost. Blaine's simple slow torture mechanism of the boot and water made me aware that if I allowed myself to give up concentrating on how it was happening as opposed to understanding how it worked, then one more fragment of my ego would drop away and his desires move that much closer to the fore. Yet I still hadn't organized my thoughts enough to comprehend why my eagerness to serve him was something he thought less important than submission in total.

"Getting myself beyond that is the challenge. I'm not sure who faces the greater chore here," I told him. "You by leading me to a point where the ego breaks off or me giving up to where I become unafraid enough to make the leap."

"The 'leap' is a big one, you are correct. But it's the one gift I can give you. An ability to see your deeper primal masculine self, meet him, if you will, without all the fucking background noise. If you go through the motions and do all the 'Sir' and 'Master' stuff superficially, you've gone through something that is as safe as an amusement park ride. I hate to admit it, but I can't empathize easily with loneliness because I've been so often pursued. What I can offer you is true strength, peace and calm, and the ability to learn to trust a Man who both protects and demands of you."

"So in effect, I become a part of you for a period of time in order to do and see different things?"

"Yes, Jim. Control is always aimed at the inner man, to allow him something powerful enough to believe in so he can truly surrender inside himself and transcend the nattering of his ego." He popped the yellow rubber of the snakebite cups from my nipples and I sucked my breath in. The warmth of the blood rushing to my chest gave those first deep feelings of pleasure/ pain mixture.

"That's hard for me, Sir, because I am one of those men who wants to be the best boy possible."

Blaine had picked up a crop and was flicking it across my swollen nipples. "As long as you are in that headset, though, you are not in submission. You're in aggression. As a result, you can't feel the inner depths of your own strength. You get distracted by 'trying.' I don't want you to 'act' submissive. I want you to know that you can submit to me, progressively, to greater levels of power in yourself." The flit-flit of the tip of Blaine's crop took on the mental ticking of a metronome, its time signature attuned from between Master's hand to me, a sightless but sexual journeyman. "Are you strong enough to drop away the shielding and feel the value of being yourself, in my service, without trying to impress me?"

The question was rhetorical, of course. I already knew that Blaine wouldn't be treating me like this if I hadn't impressed him deeply in the first place. Still, the implications of where Blaine was trying to guide me continued eluding me, like an answer written just outside my blindfold. Damn, I needed to reach that point! The pressure of his mental prodding, the gradual increase in physical torments, they kept me struggling toward the endpoint of this particular sensual quest.

With each crack of Blaine's crop, his power over me deepened as my own arousal waxed and waned at his whim. Desires tempted, needs filled, but only as he saw fit to gift me. My body trembled with the blows, causing the incremental increasing weight of the filling boot to shift and jostle. Then, a realization.

"You hit my feelings about playing outside of my relationship squarely on the head," I told him. "Despite the degree of 'care taking' being a play slave replenishes, I often feel lousy about myself afterwards and wish for more, even as I treasure the warmth from a strong ass beating. Is it humiliating? Sometimes yes. But when it seems to be the closest thing to an affectionate relationship that I know right then, it becomes – I won't even say difficult - but impossible to ignore."

Almost on cue, Blaine moved from my chest to my ass. He already knows that warm-ups are unnecessary in this zone. "I'm not trying to spoil your other contacts! You do and we all do sex sometimes for its own sake. I'm a powerful man," he punctuated the sentence with an uncommonly forceful strike to my backside. "I've learned from others, earned part of it through experience and also through embarrassing accident. I have my weaknesses and strengths. But others want strength from me and it's erotic to give it."

Pleasing warmth had crept from my buttocks and thighs and into the gray cells of my brain. The power of Blaine's dominance had once again erotically fooled my mind, even though I could already tell that the following morning would bring reds, blacks, and blues to my cheeks. I knew that I'd be reminded of his physical touch for the next several days. Mentally, I had the perception that this particular session was already forging a place for the history pages. "Sometimes when I see other men, Sir, the visit is just as much an act as it is an essential need. I always feel the most comfort when I get on my knees for them, yet often I don't 100% mean it. Do you understand what I'm trying to express?"

"I'm trying to tell you that I see you as ready for something more challenging, more erotic. Something that reflects my own deeper sense of why I do this with True Men, so hard, by the way, to find. Jim, a True Man, knows that giving up and taking in on a spiritual level will always balance, just as soon as you allow it to happen."

"At the same time, Sir, when I tell you what emotional and spiritual levels we sometimes reach, I wonder what and how much I lost or gave up for those moments."

"You alone must do what seems right with each person you include in your sexual life. I'm just telling you who I am and what I know and expect. I use the term 'sacred space' to describe it, simply because it is a place that is accessed by ritual. S/M or BD are highly ritualistic acts, Jim. The contradictions of sex, the 'feeling dirty' leads men to this kind of unwillingness to do it with people who aren't THERE on some serious level."

My blindfold was removed, and Blaine undid the cock ring and boot as well, allowing blood to freely circulate back into my balls and shaft. "What you touch upon in yourself is just as important if not more so, than anything a Master touches in you." His words and my crotch both stabbed like hell. They always did, every time, and from Blaine I lived for it. "Jim, this is what I want you to remember. The people you deal with in the scene are always important." He poured the water from the boot into a nearby basin. When he returned to me, he looked me square in the eye while painfully massaging my nipples. "How many friends have you lost in the past decade?"

"Sir, more than I can count. But everyone one of them still hurts."

"I think that you almost understand what I'm trying to pound into you," he said with an oddly gentle smile, "and I think it's time we moved on." Blaine produced a bag of clothes pins for me to see. "The lesson, Jim, is in letting go. Sometimes we forget that there are still living men standing next to us for every friend we've lost. Don't forget the ones who are gone, but every once in a while, remind yourself to celebrate the living. Remind yourself that there is balance." He lit a pair of candles and set them nearby, then dimmed the electrical lights through the room.

"There are two sides to forever, Jim. The one we exist on now and the one where we discover how far we've moved in time before coming back for the next round."

The first clothespin opened against my already sensitive chest as Blaine gripped the skin with his other hand. "As each pin closes on you, repeat the name of someone you know who has gone."

I felt the tingle as the first pinch came to close. "Wayne, Sir." Second pinch. "Ken, Sir." Third. "Jan, Sir." My litany continued on and on until a line of clothespins burned clear across my chest, down my midriff and in a circle around my heart. I could no longer control my emotions, each name and clothespin ached so deep that my tears were flowing unceasingly. All I could think of was the ache, the agonizing ache of the losses, and of the respect I had for the man drawing these emotions to skin level.

"All memories of these men are proud ones, Jim. Keep this next thought in mind; sometimes the longer you let them stay, the more painful their letting go." One by one, starting with the right side of my chest, name-pin after name-pin began coming off as I screamed to the side of forever that Blaine and I represented, tears continuing their free rain. One rubber gloved hand leaving a branded red line up my chest and to my heart, the other gently massaging my cock through the pangs of release, of the letting go. The realization that respect, control and submission remain in the hands of the living, that destiny is still just as much a plan as an accident, that what is power and what is powerful are not always the same. The reminder that the living are meant to be a source of constant celebration even as we mourn our losses.

Whatever else Blaine was whispering in my ear at that moment was gone to me, my cries blotting out all other sounds and the flaming ring around my heart branding my nerves straight to the brain, aware now only of the fire in my chest and the slippery, cool hand feverishly stroking my dick. Blaine's hand, in control, guiding me through the tiny point that was/is right now, the pilot of this journey once again taking both of us to a destination only the few can understand, accompanied by the explosion from within my balls that shoots across his glove. My sight still blurry as I realize his eyes are also a berth for tears.

My exhausted body fell into his as the warmth of that voice sobbed words of comfort, understanding, and protectiveness. Blaine undid the chain of the collar then released my wrists from the restraints behind my back and led us, spent, to his bed.

BOUNTY HUNTERS

With Brian treading water and fearful of climbing out of the pool, Malloy turned to Frank and Luke. Think of the long haul, he reminded himself. "You two are tough men," he said to Frank and Luke, playing off their arrogance. "I think I have a business idea for the three of us." When he saw their eyes light up, he knew his plan was off to a good start. The long haul, he thought again, the long haul…

Part 1: Jumper Frank Michaels

Luke and Frank downshifted the pickup they were cruising in as they searched the neighborhood. An anonymous tip to Malloy had informed them that Frank Michaels, a bond jumper for two counts of assault, had holed up in an unused apartment in the complex they were driving through. Luke slid the steering wheel through his gloves as both he and Frank kept scanning back and forth for the apartment number Michaels had allegedly hidden himself in.

Michaels also knew he was a hunted man, and he'd been keeping his eyes on the neighboring streets. When he saw the two muscle-bound men in an unfamiliar truck crawling along the cul-de-sacs, he knew he'd been made. He made a fast break back into the apartment and raced to the top of the steps. There were no furnishings, nothing there to hide in or behind, but there was a walk-in closet in the master bedroom that had a high upper shelf. Michaels hoisted himself up two levels of shelving and crammed his tight frame into the space, making himself as small as he could.

As they pulled the truck into a parking space, Luke and Frank saw the apartment number they'd been searching for and put the truck into park. There were children's toys scattered around the unit next door, but not a thing to indicate that anyone occupied their target location. After repeated attempts at knocking on the door to no response, they tried and found the door to be unlocked. Drawing their weapons, they went inside.

Moving from room to room, they popped open cabinets and closet doors, but no Michaels. Empty shower, empty bathroom. No sofas to hide behind; no beds to crawl under. Just carpet and walls, and no person to pick up. The master bedroom was the last room they got to, and Luke flipped on the light in the darker corner. He popped open the door to the walk-in closet and flicked his flashlight back and forth. Michaels squeezed himself into a tighter ball, holding his breath, but for some reason, Luke didn't look to the uppermost shelf.

"Dammit," Frank muttered under his breath, "looks like a clear house." He holstered his weapon as Luke did the same. "Let's go look out back." The two men went down the steps away from the bedroom, as Michaels held his breath in hopes that he'd soon hear a door shut to signal their exit. Michaels kept himself low, softly treading the steps and into the living room, where he peered between the blinds to see where his pursuers were. He could plainly see the broad back of a man in a Bail Enforcement t-shirt get into the pick-up. He ran to the back screen door, slid it open, and made a break for it.

But Luke and Frank had merely moved the truck to the other side of the apartment building in wait. As soon as they saw Michaels sprint across the back yard, they were on him like a pair of bloodhounds. Frank got to Michaels first, tackling him in front of a second block of buildings. Even with Frank trying to bear hug Michaels to the ground, Michaels still managed to slip away by shedding his shirt, leaving Frank holding the fabric and watching in surprise as his jumper sprinted off.

Luke was the faster of the pair and quickly caught up with the shirtless Michaels as he tried to cut through a basketball court, surrounded by a chain-link fence. He thought for a minute that he was cornered, and both Luke and Frank pulled their guns and ordered Michaels to drop to his knees. Michaels went prone, long enough to spy a small tear in the fence that he would be small enough to break through. When Luke sheathed his weapon to get out his cuffs, Michaels made another run for freedom. He popped through the hole in the fence long enough to leave Frank and Luke again shocked and forced to chase their suspect again.

This time luck was not on Michaels' side. He ran into an iron-grating fence that was locked, allowing Luke and Frank to pin him into a corner. Panting for breath, he finally got on his knees and Frank slapped a pair of handcuffs on him, and pulled him up by his elbows to walk him back to where the truck was parked, along with a man-sized, wooden crate.   Lifting him up in a fireman's carry, they dropped him into the crate as he protested. "There's a hammer and nails in the back of the truck," Luke told Frank, "I'll go get 'em. Let's box him up."

Frank pressed the top of the crate down hard across Michaels' head, and turned around just in time to see a King Country Patrol Cruiser slide up to the curb. Luke scowled as he noticed it as well. Michaels tried to take the opportunity to free himself from his predicament by yelling to the cop, "Tell 'em to let me out of here. This is harassment, man!"

Luke looked to the officer's nameplate and saw his name: Nickel. "What are y'all doing?"

"He's wanted on bail," Luke informed the officer, "he's a jumper."

"You're involved with a law enforcement agency? This guy jumped bond?"

From inside the crate, Michaels shouted again. "They're harassing me, man!"

Giving the crate a kick, Luke snarled. "You can see why he's in the crate," he explained to Nickel.

"Well, I got a complaint that you guys were running around here in camouflage with guns out," Nickel seemed confused by the turn of events. "Scaring everybody." He'd seen bounty hunters before, but never anyone who caught their skippers and then boxed them up. Something didn't seem right to him, but he didn't press it. Luke and Frank looked too intimidating to him and he didn't do well without getting orders from his superiors. "So who is he, anyway," he asked sheepishly.

"Frank Michaels. Two counts of assault."

Nickel perked up. This was a name he knew from those superiors he was all too eager to stay in the good graces with. "I'll be darned. I know him. There's somebody you need to meet concerning this boy. He'll get you a heck of a lot more money than you'd make off Michaels' bond. You interested?"

Frank and Luke exchanged glances. They'd have to clear it with Malloy but figured the opportunity for more than just a cut of the bond would get his attention, too. "Sure."

"Load him up in your truck and follow me, then."

Hoisting Michaels onto the bed of their pick-up, Luke and Frank took after the King County Cruiser. Frank pulled out his cell phone and rang up Malloy at the base of operations. "Hey. This Frank Michaels guy has some people on the lookout for him. They're willing to pay top dollar for him instead of turning him into the bondsmen. You in?"

Malloy was certainly interested. While the Bail Enforcement company he'd lured Luke and Frank into forming had been building up a reputation and a roster of clients, what he was waiting for was making enough of a killing to burn these two yokels and keep the take. He'd heard of the occasional victim who would be more than happy to compensate above the bail take for some personal restitution. Michaels sounded like he might be the ticket. "Take him into whoever offers the most," he responded.

There was a chuckle on the other end of the line. "You got it, bud," Frank shut the phone down and turned to Luke. "We could be making a real stake on this one," he chuckled. Nickel's cruiser was pulling up to a larger house behind a stone wall. The place was a serious spread across several acres, easily. The willows were blowing in the breeze across the long driveway, as Nickel's cruiser drew to a stop. From somewhere, someone lifted the automatic garage opener, allowing Luke to back the truck and its still protesting cargo inside. The door rumbled shut behind them.

Part 2: Herbert Schroeder

Luke gave the crate another good hit as Michaels kept yelling. "You like your little run, punk?" he taunted the crated man. "You got caught, didn't you?" Nickel came in through a side door.

"Come on fellas," he gestured. "There's someone upstairs I'd like you to meet." When they reached the top of the steps, a nattily dressed young man greeted the trio with a look of disdain.

"Ah, the local police," he sniffed at Nickel. He glanced at Frank and Luke. "To what do we owe the pleasure of this visit?"

Nickel visibly withered under the younger man's glare. "Well, it seems we have a little problem. These gentlemen caught Michaels trying to flee the state."

Folding his hands in front of him, the butler looked over to the bail enforcers. "I think the boss might be interested in hearing about this. One moment please." He spun on his heel and vanished behind one of the twin sets of dark mahogany doors in the foyer.

"Nice house," Luke leered, as the door opened to reveal another sharply dressed, tall blond man in creased pants and suspenders. His hands were working on the barrel of a pistol that Luke recognized. "A P-38 Luger?"

"Yes it is," the tall man answered. "Gentlemen! What can I do for you?"

Frank couldn't resist a dig at the formality of the butler and the master of the mansion. "P-38? We used these for can-openers in the army."

The Lord of The Manor was unperturbed. "It's been in my family for generations. It belonged to my grandfather. He was a proud German."

The butler was adept enough to smell a situation that needed defusing before it went too far. He deftly broke into the conversation by advising his boss. "These, uh, gentlemen, caught Mr. Michaels trying to flee the state. And they have him downstairs in... what is it?"

Luke was beginning to feel a growing disdain for the situation, but could smell the money that this man and his attitude exuded. "A crate," he snorted.

"Yes," the butler snorted in return. "A crate."

The Boss perked up. "He always was a sneaky little bastard. Where'd you find him?"

Luke watched as Nickel moved into a position behind him and Luke. These two were a piece of work, he thought. They'd obviously turned Nickel into their own personal pussy-cop, and weren't used to not getting their own way. Which meant that Michaels was worth more than they wanted to let on, but they wanted him. They wanted him real bad. "We caught him trying to jump bail. He was holed up in an apartment complex."

The boss holstered the Luger. "I think we have some business to discuss." He motioned for the butler to open the second set of doors. "This way, gentlemen." The room was filled with solid oak desk furniture and a variety of antiques. He gestured for Luke and Frank to sit down, ignoring Nickel entirely. It was a gesture not lost on Frank and Luke; the cop was a disposable commodity. Taking a seat behind the broad desk, the boss took the moment to introduce himself. "I'm Herbert

Schroeder. That man you have downstairs, Frank Michaels, is one of three men who embezzled roughly a million-five from one of my construction firms. The first one I already caught on my own. He gave up Michaels before he had an unfortunate accident at a construction site. There's one more that I know of, maybe more, and I still haven't found out where they have the money or what they've done with it. You two get Michaels to give up his partner and the money and I'll give you 20% for you to split."

There was a pause and Luke and Frank briefly thought the situation through. Twenty percent meant a take of over $200,000 to split three ways with Malloy, but Schroeder had already essentially admitted to killing one person. How far could they trust him? Frank was too greedy to resist the pull for too long, chipping in first. "We're in." Luke reluctantly nodded in agreement as Schroeder broke into a wide, white smile.

"Good, gentlemen," he said with a laugh. "Let's go down to your crate and get started." He waved for the butler to get Nickel out of the room, and the cop scurried off obediently. However, he led Luke and Frank down the steps to the garage, where Michaels was still boarded up behind the slats of the oversized packing crate.

"Well Michaels," Schroeder said, sidling up to the side of the truck. "Guess you'd forgotten about me, didn't you?" Michaels was suddenly silent, finally realizing where the two bounty hunters had really brought him. "Now, I'm not mad at you, I'm not upset with you. I just want to know where your buddies are and where the money is. That's all I want to know."

Michaels wasn't bright enough to determine that he wasn't in much of a position to negotiate, but he still snarled at Schroeder and refused to cooperate. "I ain't telling you shit," he drawled, "Screw you, pretty boy."

"Michaels, you're gonna piss me off." This time, Michaels spit through the crate boards. Schroeder immediately flew into a rage. "Shut the fuck up, Michaels. You're going to tell me exactly what I want to know. Damn you! I want that money, I want your friends, and I want them right fucking now!"

"I ain't telling you nothing."

Schroeder was practically spitting in anger at this point. "That's it! All right guys. You two take him inside, leave him in the crate, and we'll deal with him. Now, dammit!"

Frank and Luke picked up the crate and began sliding it off the truck bed. Perhaps too late, Michaels realized that this wasn't going to go his way. "What are you going to do?" he whimpered.

"You had your chance, Michaels, now it's my turn."

The butler directed Frank and Luke to slide the crate into an adjoining room. The space was an elaborate workshop, with plenty of tools all racked against the wall in a perfect working order, a huge, sturdy table in the center with industrial clamps on each end, and cabinets for additional power tools against the walls. Schroeder was still spitting mad that Michaels was openly defying him and had no intention of letting such an indignity stand.

"Get him alongside the table and get that crate open," Schroeder demanded. As Frank and Luke pried the boards from the top of the crate, the butler appeared with two long leather straps with cuffs on the end, and tossed them across the length of the table. Without missing a beat, he had Michaels' hands restrained and the captive pulled across the table. Another set of cuffs was put around his ankles and Michaels was securely stretched across the table, bent over at the waist. Schroeder looked at his wall of tools and selected a ball-peen hammer.

"You'll tell me where the money is and who else was in on this, and you'll tell me now," he sneered.

Michaels still refused to say anything but "fuck you" to Schroeder, who answered by taking one of Michaels' fingers and, with one swift slam, bashed the ball-peen hammer across the knuckle. Frank and Luke stood back in shock. But they knew that Michaels was not going to be an easy crack, and they'd have to stand by if they wanted any chance at the missing money.

Howling in pain at the sight of his mangled finger, Michaels began taking the situation seriously. "I don't know, man, don't know!" he wailed. That answer did not satisfy Schroeder, who pulled another finger out from the cuffed wrists and laid down another crack, letting the ball of the hammer pulverize a second of Michaels' fingers. A scream filled the room, then sobs. "Tim Stevens! It was Tim Stevens!" Michaels broke down in wracked sobs, still pulled shirtless across the table.

"Where's the money!" Schroeder ordered, "Where's the goddamn money?" He took Michaels' hand and pulled it flat across the flat hard wood, and prepared to smash the hammer directly into the palm.

Michaels screamed before the hammer had a chance to fall. "Stevens has it! It was just the three of us, I swear!" Schroeder drew the hammer back from Michaels' hand.

He slid the hammer across the table to his butler, who scooped it from the table and stood with Frank and Luke. Schroeder leaned across the table to get face to face with Michaels. "Just you, Stevens and Charlie then? And Stevens has the money?" Through his wails, Michaels nodded in agreement. Recalling what Schroeder had said earlier about a 'construction accident,' Frank and Luke already knew what happened to Charlie. But then Schroeder gave a nod to the butler, who hauled back and gave the ball-peen a mighty swing into the back of Michaels' skull. He retracted his arm and laid in with a second, sickening crack, splitting Michaels' head wide open with splatter barely missing Frank and Luke. Schroeder stood across the table, totally unfazed by the bloody mess laid out in front of him. He tossed his head again at his butler and said "Clean this up" about as off-handedly as he would have said "walk the dogs" and with probably less empathy. He shot a look at Frank and Luke. "This Tim Stevens guy lives in southern King County. You two find him and get him to me. If he knows where the money is, he'll give it up."

All Frank and Luke could do was stare in amazement. Before this, they were bounty hunters looking for a quick score on the side. Now they were accessories to murder. It was too deep to back out now.

Part 3: Jumper Tim Stevens

Having picked up the address of Stevens from Schroeder's cop-lackey Nickel, Frank and Luke had already scouted out the house Stevens was supposed to be living in. As it turned out, he also had outstanding warrants for petty crimes and had been put on a list for skipping bail. It was early morning when they picked the lock and made their way up the front steps to where they assumed the master bedroom would be. Luke put his finger to his lips to signal for quiet; he and Frank could hear the rush of a shower running at the top of the stairs. A look around the doorframe revealed the outlines of a naked Stevens behind the frosted glass and steaming water.

Stevens exited the shower and grabbed a towel. He was drying off his hair when he heard the sound behind him. "Get on the floor! On your knees!" bellowed Luke. Stevens, in shock, dropped the towel and fell to his knees. "Get your hands on your head!"

Frank grabbed one wrist and slapped the cuffs on that one first, then twisted the opposite wrist down where he could slap the second cuff down hard across Stevens' bone. "What the hell are y'all doing in my house? Who told you where I was at?"

"Shut up," retorted Luke, "You thought you'd get away with skirting this bail, didn't you? You don't skip on us." They picked up Stevens' naked body and threw it across the bed. Frank jumped across the mattress and began drilling Stevens' ribs with his SAP gloves.

"I did," snapped Stevens. "I'll do it again. I'm gonna have y'all's ass for getting in my house."

With another punch into Stevens' side, Frank laughed. "I don't think so."

Luke chimed in, "What are you gonna do? You're the one in the cuffs."

"I got away once... Ugghh!" Stevens kept trying to backtalk but couldn't stop the steady stream of punches to his gut. "All right! Let me put some clothes on!"

Taking note of just how hairy Stevens was, Frank snickered. "Where do you think you are, monkey boy? You ain't getting any clothes. This ain't some Holiday Inn, where do you think you're at?"

"It's my house! I'll have your job for getting in here."

Luke laughed. "If this is your house, how'd we get in it? This probably isn't your house; you can't even prove it." He slapped Stevens across the face. "You ain't nothing.

Remember your buddies? Remember Michaels? Your friends are the ones who dropped the dime on you."

Stevens' nose and lip were bleeding from the constant slaps. "Yeah, Michaels. I know that little fuckstick. He's the one who told you where I was at, didn't he?"

Frank continued. "Remember Charlie. Yeah, remember Charlie? We got him, too." 'Even if he's under some building's foundation,' he thought. "Now how about the money you took from Schroeder?"

"Okay, okay I'll go," Stevens begged. He was worn out by the barrage of punches and slaps, and could taste the blood in his mouth. "Just let me put some clothes on. Can't we make a deal?"

"A deal," Luke laughed again, "a deal? Now he's trying to bribe us!" He let loose with another series of sternum hits before pulling his arms up behind his back. "Let's go." Frank and Luke hooked their arms under Stevens' and hauled him out to their awaiting Jeep. "We got a friend who's really good at getting answers." Opening the hatch, they pushed Stevens' nude and cuffed body across the bed of the Jeep.

Luck was not going their way this time. As they were headed back to home base, a King County Cruiser pulled up behind them with lights flashing. "Jesus," muttered Frank. "Here comes another one of those real cops." The officer exited his vehicle and wandered up to the side of the Jeep. Stevens was thrashing around enough that the cop must have seen him through the back windows.

"You mind explaining to me why you got a naked man in the back of your truck?" he asked incredulously.

Frank pointed to the front of Luke's shirt. "Can you read his shirt right there? Can you see that?"

"Don't get smart with me," the cop snapped.

"Bail enforcement," Luke cut in. "He's one of our bond jumpers."

"Bond jumpers. And who is he?"

"Tim Stevens"

The cop already knew about Stevens' problems with Schroeder. Turning him in would make some points at headquarters. "You nabbed Tim Stevens. Good work. I'll take care of him for right now, I'll take over."

Frank stopped him mid-sentence. "No, no. This one's ours."

Luke wasn't going to let this potential score get away. "What makes you think you're going to take away our man."

"That's our bread and butter," Frank jabbed, "genius."

The cop was getting angry. "Shut up, mouth." He pointed at his shirt this time. "That says 'Law Enforcement Officer.' Get out of the car." Reluctantly, Frank and Luke got out of the Jeep. "Put 'em up! Put your hands on the car!" When the cop went back to his cruiser to radio in, Luke decided he wasn't going to let this punk steal their bread and butter out from under them.

Luke pulled his weapon and aimed it at the cop. "Why don't you step away from the vehicle. How about that, smart guy. Now, come back here."

Taken totally off guard, the cop pushed the patrol car door shut. "You men are making a big mistake," he sputtered.

"Keep your hands away from your weapon," Luke warned him, "and come here now."

The cop knew this was getting out of control, and tried to talk his way out of it. "Put your weapons down," he advised. "I'm gonna give you a chance to put your weapons down."

Cocking his gun, Luke admonished the cop. "You're in no position. You get down on your knees."

Frank had drawn his weapon as well, and had rounded the rear of the Jeep. "On your knees and lace your fingers behind your head," he snarked. "I'm sure you've told plenty of people that before." As the cop wrapped his hands behind his head, Frank taunted "Outstanding, Einstein."

"It's a federal offence," the cop warned. "40 years."

"And who is going to get us?" Luke asked.

Frank chuckled, "We'll have so much money that we won't even be in America."

"You won't be able to spend your money when you're in jail, asshole," the cop snarled as Luke cuffed his hands behind his back. "You're making a bad move. I radioed before the stop. You got law enforcement officials coming as we speak."

Frank and Luke also knew that the law officer who'd respond to the call would either be Nickel, who was on the take, or Malloy, who was on Motorcycle division today. So Frank felt no threat as he pushed the cop over. "Outstanding. That means you're doing your job." The pair lifted the cop off the ground and pushed him towards the back of the cruiser. Luke popped the trunk open as the cop began to put up a serious fight.

"I ain't going in the trunk! Let go of me"

"Sure" replied Luke, as he dropped the cop into the well of the trunk, and slammed the lid closed. "You take the Jeep and I'll get this one," he told Frank as the cop shouted protests. He flipped open his cell phone and called Malloy. "You on duty?" He queried. "Good. Meet us at your place."

Frank and Luke had already at arrived when Malloy pulled up on his motorcycle. The first thing he could hear when he shut down the engine was the cop shouting from the trunk of the cruiser. The rev from the cycle had alerted the cop that another police officer had arrived. He began yelling for help, even louder.

"He thinks you're here to help him," Luke chuckled. There's a reason I called you to this location. We got a problem. We got stopped on the way over here. We got a real cop. He's the one in the trunk."

"Well, I'm here to help you," Malloy replied.

"I think he called it in to the dispatcher," Luke continued. "Can you handle that for us?"

"Yeah," Malloy decided. "I'm in pretty tight with dispatch so I can get this one off the records."

"But can you dispose of him for us?"

"I can take care of him, too," Malloy replied. "What have we got over here?"

Luke pointed to the Jeep, where Stevens was putting forth a fresh set of cries for help. "Over here we've got our little bond jumper. The one Schroeder told us about. Tim Stevens. He knows where the money's at but he's not giving up the location. That's where you come in. You got those little ways of doing that."

Malloy smiled knowingly. "We can get that out of him."

"We slapped him around, beat him up a little bit," Luke acknowledged, "but we didn't come up with anything."

This was just what Malloy wanted to hear. If he could get the money out of Stevens while Frank and Luke took care of other loose ends, this might well play into his longer term goals. "You want me to take him to the special place? You guys going to assist me?"

Luke opened the back of the Jeep, where a naked Stevens was still cuffed. "Sure we can," he laughed as he and Frank pulled Stevens out of the back and into the garage. There was an open drainage pit in the floor, which Luke and

Frank began dragging Stevens toward. The pushed him down feet first, using their boots on his shoulders to get him the rest of the way down. It took the two of them to slide the iron grate over the hole to cover Stevens in the pit.

"Let me out," Stevens kept yelling, even as Frank and Luke kept stepping on his fingers as he tried to push the grate up.

"It took two of us to pull that grate over," Luke spoke down to the captive, "I don't think you're going to get it up yourself."

Frank hocked up a spitball and let it fly. "Don't be spitting on me!"

"I may not be spitting on you," Frank retorted. "But I think I may have something special for you a little later," as he again used his boots across Stevens' fingers. "Keep them down there if you want them whole!"

"Don't put them up there, dumbass," Luke taunted as Stevens yelped in pain.

Frank reached for his fly. "You know, I'm feeling a sudden urge…" He pulled his cock out and let loose with a full-on stream of piss. It shot through the bars of the grate as Stevens screamed and tried in vain to dodge the liquid as it poured down across him and into the drain below. Luke decided it was time to bring the cruiser in after this episode and went outside. Pulling the patrol car into the garage, he parked the front wheel across the grate to make sure that there would be no way for Stevens to even have a chance to push himself out.

Malloy came back in, mirror shades still on despite being in the garage. "What do you have in here?"

"That's Tim. That's our pit-boy," Luke replied.

"Get your face up here where I can see you," Malloy ordered. "You having a good time in there?"

"Hell no," Stevens whimpered." I want out. They put this car on top of me like I'm going to go somewhere."

Malloy glanced back and forth between Luke and Frank. "The usual story. They never know anything." He bent down to get a better look. "Just tell us where the money's at."

"I'm not going to tell you where the money's at. I don't know"

Breathing a heavy sigh, Malloy asked "How long has he been down there?"

"Been a pretty good while," Luke replied.

Kneeling back over the grated pit, Malloy faced Stevens from above. "I've got a special place to take you. I bet you when I get done with you today you'll tell me where it's at."

Part 4: Convincing The Cop

Leaving Stevens to stew in the pit, Luke, Frank and Malloy turned their attentions to the cop who was still in the trunk of the cruiser. Popping the trunk, they grabbed him by hooking him under his elbows as he vehemently protested. Pushing him through a side door, the cop got shoved face first into a wall. Frank and Luke began to pummel him with their gloved fists. They rained blows into his sides and then his stomach, as Malloy stood behind them, taunting, "Soften him up a little before we put him in the bubble."

The blows continued as the hits to the sternum finally caused the cop to have a coughing seizure. "What's the matter, boy," Luke sneered, "having trouble breathing?" Wait till you see what's in the next room. Oh yeah, and look at this." He forced the cop to stare directly into Malloy's mirrored shades.

"You traitor," the cop seethed, "You fucking traitor!"

Malloy just laughed. "I already called dispatch. Your little call is already off the records. No one knows you're here, no one knows you got picked up. You'll forget all about this, understand?" He grabbed the cop in his gloved hand and squeezed his face. "I'll see you later."

Malloy and Frank grabbed the cop and pulled him into the next room. There was a stretcher set up across a huge plastic sort of tarp, and that was where Frank and Luke were pushing him. Driving his body across the stretcher rails, they uncuffed his hands behind his back before clamping one wrist to the side rail. Pulling a second set of cuffs, the opposite wrist was secured to the other side of the stretcher. As they rolled him across the stretcher, they began to pull straps from the sides and secured them across the cop's body.

These were strong straps, woven out of strong nylon, meant to make sure patients in transit didn't get rolled off the stretcher in case of accidents in the ambulance. Pulled tight and fastened across the cop's legs, it was certain he wasn't going to have much room to squirm. Another band was tightened across his chest, then a neck and chin brace was locked into place around his head.

Then came the part that filled the cop with terror. "Remember what we said about having trouble breathing?" Luke grabbed a sheet of the plastic and pulled it over the stretcher and the cop's head. "What do you think happens now?" Luke and Frank started to pull a zipper around the base of the stretcher, along a silver base that the stretcher was parked on top of.

"Wait! I'll do anything! I won't be able to breathe," the cop screamed. He could hear a little buzz as a fan was turned on behind him, and he felt air blowing into his back. But he also had to fight off the approaches of Frank, who kept pulling the plastic tight over his face, cutting off his air. He started to choke, and Frank would let up just long enough to let him catch his breath, and then do it again. Even as the cocoon continued to inflate, the cop kept feeling his air passage getting choked off mercilessly.

"You're here until we let you out," Luke advised him. "If your fellow cop says you'll keep your mouth shut, he'll let you out. If not," this time he pressed his gloved hands across the cop's nose and mouth, "we turn off the fan and leave you inside the plastic baggie here." The temporary quarantine bubble hummed as the cop began yelling for help. It didn't matter, as Luke and Frank hi-fived each other as they left the cop inside the cocoon, his boots kicking at the plastic, begging for someone to let him out.

Part 5: The Butler

With Stevens in Malloy's hands, Frank and Luke decided to make another round at Schroeder's mansion to report their progress. They had no doubts that Malloy's special skills would net them the location of the missing money. After all, Frank could remember the number he'd done to Brian, enough so that Brian had up and run away at the suggestion that Malloy, Frank and he were about to start a bail enforcement company.

But when they entered, they found the snotty butler at the top of the stairs, playing with a radio-controlled car. "Well, my friends the bounty hunters. How are you gentlemen?"

Frank and Luke were already feeling the hair stand up on the back of their necks. "Wonderful," Frank snarled. Luke just glowered.

"A situation has arisen," he told Frank and Luke, "that can benefit the both of us. The Boss has decided to cut you out of the deal."

Luke continued to stare angrily. "That just not gonna work," he growled.

"If we work together, we can take care of this," the Butler explained. "He's kind of difficult to get to sometimes, but if you get the information about where the money is, give me a call. I'll help you get to the Boss."

Luke didn't trust the little weasel, but he played along. "What you're saying is... you'll take care of us while you're going to go behind your boss's back."

"Let's just say I'm tired of being the second man." The Butler fondled the electric car remote nervously. "It's about time I got a piece of the action."

"So we're going to work for you?"

"Let's just say we'll work together." The Butler extended his hand to Luke. "Deal?"

Luke put his gloved hand into the Butler's. "That'll work." The Butler shook Frank's hand as well. "Let's get to work then."

As the Butler went back to playing with his electronic car, Frank and Luke headed back to their car. "Trust him?" Frank asked.

"About as far as I can spit," Luke answered. "You saw what he did to Michaels' head. He'll split ours even faster if he gets the chance."

Frank thought for a moment. "He may be double-crossing his boss, but I think we're going to get this entire one." He mulled it over a few more moments. "Yeah. We're going for all of it."

Part 6: Stevens in the Special Place

Malloy had completed his ritual. His prey was finally out of the pit, and handcuffed on the floor of his bathroom. The sting of hot water had washed him into a purer state so now that he was ready to take his prey, he'd be a clean god. It had been a while; in fact, it was Luke's punk brother Brian who'd been the last person on that floor. He didn't even get the chance to fuck him, and that asshole Luke had raped him thinking it was revenge. The long haul, he reminded himself, and this kid may be the answer.

He was pulling a clean uniform over his newly cleansed body as he expanded his chest. And this Stevens dude had a hot ass. Once they got the money out of him and given him a good ass-whupping, he may just have to take a go at it. As for Frank and Luke, they'd find out how patient he could be when it came to payback.

Pulling his boots over his leggings, he pushed a heel into Stevens' butt cheeks. Stevens groaned into the gag Malloy had stuffed into his mouth to keep him quiet during his ritual. This hairy little fuck is going to love my basement, he thought. Getting him to spill his guts would be easier if Luke and Frank weren't around. They were amateurs when it came to breaking men down. A scowl creased his face. If this little shit gives up the money, then Frank and Luke were in for a bigger surprise than this kid was going to find.

He yanked the gag out of Stevens' mouth and pulled him to his feet. Getting a chokehold from behind, Malloy began forcing Stevens down the stairwell to the basement. "I got a surprise for you," he taunted.

"Nothing can surprise me," Stevens snapped back. "I've been through it all."

Opening the basement door, Malloy laughed. "This is my room, boy."

Taking in all the chains and cuffs, all the floggers and whips, Stevens tensed up immediately. "What the hell kind of place is this!" Malloy pushed him into a wooden frame and undid the handcuffs, whipping Stevens' wrist over his head and recuffing the wrist to a length of chain, then pulling a second set of cuffs and restraining Stevens' other wrist to an opposite chain. "What kind of sick place is this," he said, his voice now rising in a panic.

"Don't you worry about that. You're going to find out soon enough." Slapping Stevens across the face, Malloy went to the next room and began to organize his equipment. He heard the door open from the stairwell. Oh shit, he thought, here come the amateurs. But he smiled as Frank and Luke came into the room and greeted them. "I gotta go out for a moment and get some equipment," he said. "I'll be right back. Got your boy over there," he nodded, indicating the frame where Stevens was dangling from the handcuffs.

Luke heard the door close behind Malloy as they went to Stevens in the frame. Grabbing Stevens by the jaw, he stared right into his face and snarled "Remember that conversation we had? Remember that conversation?" He squeezed Stevens' jaw tighter in his gloved hands. "About the money?"

"I remember," Stevens gasped.

"Anything come to mind about it?" Luke let a punch land in Stevens' gut. "Remember anything about the money?"

Doubled over, Stevens said "I'm not telling you about the money. I don't know!"

Frank selected a flogger off the wall of Malloy's tools. Its long red leather tails rustled through his hands. Stevens found himself chest to chest with Luke as Frank stood behind him. "Now, one more time," Luke said softly. "This is the plan. That cop brought you in here? We don't really care about splitting the money with him. It's just between me and him," he said, pointing to Frank. "So you're going to tell us where the money's at."

Stevens was still resistant, shouting "No!"

"Hold his head down," Frank said from behind Stevens. Luke put Stevens' head in a choke and bent his forehead into his shoulders. "You sure?" Then Frank drew back and let the flogger crack down on Stevens' back. He let the blows rain down while Luke kept demanding information. They knew if they could get the location before Malloy came back, they could get the cash and skip on Malloy and Schroeder. But Malloy was right; Frank and Luke's interrogation skills weren't as keen as Malloy's. They could deliver a beatdown but nothing that could really break someone's resolve.

Not that Frank was going to stop trying. He clenched his gloved fist around a handful of Stevens' chest hair and began twisting and pulling. This was the most intense pain Stevens had felt since being caught and he let out a wailing scream. Thinking he might be on to something, Frank did it again. "Hell no! No!" Stevens cried out as Frank ripped another fistful of hairs out of Stevens' skin. The next time, however, Frank aimed lower, and clutched just above Stevens' cock, pulling and twisting and a handful of pubic hairs and jerking them out as hard as he could. This pain was so intense that Stevens came close to blacking out, which was when Luke stepped back in.

Patting him on the face with his glove, Luke admonished, "Don't you go to sleep on us now." Frank waved his gloves in the air and let the tiny hairs float to the ground. "Come on," he said, letting the glove hit harder each time. "Let's hear it. Let's hear it." Frustrated to his limit, Luke pulled his gun and wedged it into Stevens' mouth. "Let's hear it! Let's hear it now!"

Malloy came back in as Luke was jamming his weapon at Stevens. This was exactly the sort of thing that pissed him off, knowing that Stevens now basically thought he was dead anyway, and would be a lot harder to get talking. He glowered at Luke until he took down the gun and put it back in the holster. He kept the stare down in place until Luke turned away, then asked "Did he tell you anything?"

"Just a bunch of weenie ass little hollering."

Malloy picked up a pair of leather chaps lined up and down with D-Rings, and waved it at Stevens. "You're gonna wear these. They're just your size, too."

"They sure are purty," Luke drawled as he and Malloy started pulling them across Stevens' legs.

Stevens began to struggle in his chains and protest. "They ain't got no bottom in them!"

"You won't need a bottom for this," Luke responded as he tightened up the buckles on the front and back, and zippered the leather from inside each leg.

Malloy came around with a matching shirt. There was a series of D-Rings along the arms and across the shoulders and side, and Malloy pulled it across Stevens' chest. Forcing him up on a standing stool, Malloy pulled the belts tight across the shirt and forced Steven's uncuffed hands down each sleeve.

He produced several coils of rope and first tied the D-Rings on the wrists into the wood frame, stretching Stevens' arms apart. Then, like they were spinning a web, Malloy and Luke threaded the ropes through each D-Ring and into holes that ran down the length of the beams in the frame, slowly hoisting Stevens into the air. Malloy gave the standing stool a sharp kick and Stevens was left swinging in the maze of ropes, hanging in the air and centered between the front two pillars of the frame.

"That's a work of art, isn't it," Frank said.

Malloy nodded. "Sure is. Let him hang here for a couple hours and he'll tell us."

Stevens was suspended like an insect in a spider's web. The ropes were spun all around the frame through the series of D-Rings, leaving him to dangle, exposed, to Luke and Malloy. He was already feeling the stretch on his arms, like his circulation was being cut off. Frank had come back in to help with the finishing touches, tightening the ropes until there was little room to even squirm.

"We're gonna get some answers now," Malloy sneered. "I've been waiting for a chance to use this." He produced a leather hood and pulled it over Stevens' head. "Give it a good cinching up," he ordered Frank.

"Anything but that," Stevens protested. I can't see!"

"That's the point," Frank replied. He pulled down a flogger and Malloy did the same. The two of them began to beat Stevens from front and back, double-teaming him until the screams filled the room.

Luke interrupted and stopped Malloy. "Give us a minute."

"You got some business to take care of?"

"Yeah," he responded. "I think he's ripe."

Malloy scowled inwardly. This was his space, and he didn't take well to being told how to act. But he wanted Stevens for his own purposes and decided that if he could get rid of these two muscle heads, he'd get his time. Plus, if they knew where the money was, they'd be hot to find it, and, he assumed, Schroeder and his weasel of a butler. "You treat him for me, you hear?"

"No problem," Luke told him. Once Malloy left the room, Luke grabbed Stevens by the chin of the hood. "I bet you a cold drink of water would be really good right now," he teased. We'll let you down, get you some nice water…"

Stevens jerked in the rope web, "The money?"

"What do you think we've been talking about for the last hour?" Luke said, slapping Stevens across the mouth.

Frank picked the flogger back up and started laying into Stevens' back again. "Oooo! Quit! I'll tell you!"

The flogging stopped and Luke moved in close. "Where's the money?"

Gasping for air, Stevens broke. "The money, it's in a red house. It's on Buford Highway, right behind the Flea market. It's there. Right behind it."

Luke grabbed Stevens by the neck, "You lying to me? If you are, I'll come back and pop a round in you. I'll waste you easy."

"Yeah, now let me down! I told you where it was!"

"Not now," Luke laughed. "We're gonna send your buddy back in to play with you for a little while." Luke and Frank walked out of the room as Stevens pleaded for them to let him down off the frame.

Malloy wasted no time in getting back in the room. "It's me. How you doing in there?"

"Let me down," Stevens begged. "I told them where the money was."

Malloy scoffed. "I don't care about the money. I'm not done with you. You'll stay at my place for a while. You thought I'd bring you over here just to turn you loose?" He stepped over to the wall and selected his heaviest flogger.

"Where you at?" Stevens whimpered.

"Why are you worried about where I'm at?" as he let the flogger swing at Stevens' chest. There was a hard crack of leather on leather. Stevens cried out, his body still sore from the earlier beatings and Malloy was hitting even harder than Frank and Luke had. "You'll know where I'm at," as he took another swing across Stevens' back this time. "You'll learn to like it after a while, if you get to leave." Malloy let another round of swings across Steven's upper body. "You learning to like it yet?"

As Stevens screamed in agony, Malloy grabbed the hood at the chin. Stevens began to plead for mercy. "Yes, yes, please."

"Yes, what?"

"Yes, Sir"

Malloy chuckled low, "You'll learn a little respect while you're here. You can scream all you want, but nobody can hear us down here. I like having visitors. I appreciate you volunteering."

By now, Stevens knew he wasn't getting down from the frame. He was worried that this cop was going to kill him, but not before making him suffer for a long time, He felt Malloy's hands at the back of his head, and the hood loosen from behind. He could now see Malloy, in full uniform and helmet, mirror shades reflecting.

"You like having my hood, don't you?"

"No, I didn't like it," Stevens responded, fearing the sight of the officer in uniform.

Grabbing the flogger again, Malloy took more swings, this time at Stevens' back. "Sure like this too, don't you?"

"Please, no more," Stevens begged, "I told you where the money was!"

Malloy laughed. "What did I tell you earlier? I don't care where the money is. I'll get my part of it. And you happen to be my special guest for a while." He let the flogger fly across Stevens' back and ass. "You like that, don't you?"

"No, no please, oh god, no!" as the flogging continued. After a pronged continuous attack across his back and ass, Malloy came around front.

"You want me to quit now?"

Stevens hoped for the best, "Yes, yes."

"What did I tell you about respect," Malloy taunted as he let the flogger strike across Stevens' chest a few more times.

Screaming in response, Stevens pleaded "Sir, yes Sir, please Sir, quit, Sir, please quit, Sir!"

"That's more like it," Malloy replied. He kept hitting Stevens as he circled the frame. "I'll let you down in a little while. But when I'm down in my special place, I kind of lose track of time." The flogger kept cracking, as he continued. "So a little while could mean a couple days. Or longer." Malloy kept hitting Stevens' ass. He remembered his missed chance at Brian's and knew he wasn't going to miss his shot at a solid fuck this time. "You're not very smart are you? I think that'll be enough for a little while. I'll come back and play a little more. You'd like that, wouldn't you?"

Stevens was too defeated to try and talk back. "Yes, Sir." He meekly replied.

"All right! I'll see you in a few." Leaving Stevens dangling in the web, Malloy left to get some lube and a condom. He'd be back for more, all right, he thought.

Part 7: Schroeder's place

It had been a tough round at the gym, but Schroeder felt pumped. He let the top down on the Corvette just to let the air breeze across his bare chest, as he pulled up the driveway to his mansion. The adrenaline was still moving as he opened the front door, only to be greeted by a man in a gas mask pointing a pistol directly at his face.

"Welcome home," the masked man said. "Come on in."

Schroeder froze. "Who the hell are you guys? What are you doing in my house?"

Frank was also there, wearing a gas mask to cover his face. "Hold still, right there," he ordered.

"What I want you to do," Luke demanded, "is strip down. Now!"

"You're going to pay for this," Schroeder sniped, as he pulled his shorts down.

"You fail to understand something here, genius," Frank retorted. "We want everything off. The only thing we want to see is a vertical smile. Now move!" After Schroeder had stripped buck naked, Frank waved his gun towards the hallway. Get your face back there."

Luke and Frank marched Schroeder to the living room, where Schroeder saw his Butler hog tied on the floor, but not moving. "What the hell!" Schroeder exclaimed. He realized suddenly that the Butler wasn't breathing, and that these two psychos were deadly. "What are you fuckers going to do? That was when Frank and Luke took off their gas masks and Schroeder realized who had taken him. "What are you fucking weirdos doing?"

Luke pushed Schroeder across a couch and pinned his hands behind his back. Pulling rope from their duffle bag, they started to tie Schroeder in a hog tie like the Butler, pulling his arms together at the elbows and his ankles up to his wrists. "You guys are gonna be hunted like you never thought possible for this," Schroeder warned. "Who's paying you to do this? Who are you working with?"

"You ask a lot of questions," Luke replied, "for someone in your position. In fact, you're in a bad position. Who's this over on the floor, you know him?"

"You know I know I do."

"Well, he's the one who gave you up." Luke sneered. "And you can see what that got him. We're gonna take anything we want, you understand? Stevens gave up the money, your Butler gave you up, and you were going to double-cross us? You figured it out yet? We're fixing to kill you."

"Come on," Schroeder pleaded. "I'll double whatever you got. Anything you want." Frank and Luke hoisted him off the couch, tossing him over Franks' shoulders.

"We're fixing to dunk your ass. I want to hear you scream when we throw you in your pool," Luke whispered in his ear. "Who's the smart person now?" They carried him outside to the edge of the pool. "Let me hear you scream... on three." Frank took him off the shoulder and the two men swung him into the water. Schroeder went in with a huge splash, but didn't come up. Frank and Luke watched and waited till they were sure he was going to stay down.

Frank turned to Luke. "Nobody," Frank leered, "fucks us over."

Part 8: The Long Haul

Malloy strolled into the kitchen at their headquarters, where Frank and Luke were seated with the two duffle bags they'd found with Stevens' directions before they took care of Schroeder and the Butler. "You guys taking a trip?"

"Yeah, we got a little money to spend, "Frank said. We're thinking of Cancun."

"This divided up or is it still in a lump? You gonna split it with me or wait until you come back?"

"It's still in a lump. We figured we'd give you your share when we got back."

That was when Malloy pulled his sidearm. "Why don't you guys take out your guns and put them on the table."

Shocked, Frank and Luke took their weapons out and slid them across the table. "Guess I can't argue with that," Frank sighed.

Malloy scooped up the guns and stuck them inside one of the duffels.

Frank fumed, looking down at the table. "You just going to keep the money for yourself?"

"That's exactly what I'm going to do." He pulled out a pair of handcuffs and slid them across the table to Frank. "Put these on your buddy."

"What's up with this," Luke asked.

"I don't know," Frank replied, but when you've got a gun pointed at you, you don't argue too much." Frank clicked the cuffs across Luke's wrists.

"I know how you guys operate," Malloy said in retort. He walked the pair of bounty hunters into the next room and made

Luke sit in the chair, then pointed at the floor. Gesturing at Frank, he ordered, "Get over on the other side of the chair and get on your knees. Get your hands behind your back." When Frank did as he was told, Malloy got out a second set of cuffs and locked Frank's hands behind his back. Malloy took the duffle bag that Frank and Luke had filled with ropes and began to pull out cords.

"So you're going to tie me up?" Frank asked.

"Yeah, I'm gonna tie you up. I'm going to give myself enough time to get out of here. Remember your little brother Brian? You should have listened to him instead of me when he said I shouldn't be trusted. I've been waiting for this moment ever since you fucked me in my own house."

"You're gonna keep the money for yourself now over that? After all we did together?"

"Hell yeah," Malloy replied. "I work on things for a long time, and that included getting you back for that night." He turned to Frank and began to tie his ankles. "All I wanted to do was get one good opportunity to leave you guys wondering what I did to you and take all the earnings. There's over a million in those bags. I cleaned out the safe, too. By the time you two get loose, I'll be halfway to Mexico." He finished hogtieing Frank and made certain his ankles were pulled up tight to his wrists. "You better not roll over," he warned. "Or you might have some trouble breathing."

"You better spend your money fast," Frank warned, "because we will track you down."

"Let's weigh in on your situation," Malloy sneered. "I'll call in this situation when I touch down tonight. In North King County, my guess is they'll find Schroeder and that weasel face of a Butler dead. Stevens is back at my place fucked like a dog and put away in a cage wet. There's a cop chained to a gurney in a quarantine bubble. When the cops find all of them, my guess is you'll have too much to explain for than worrying about me and where the money went." He finished tying the knots to hold Luke in the chair. "When I want to get revenge," he cracked, "I can wait a long time and make sure it burns you worse than anything you ever did to me. I get into things for the long haul, buddy. You fucked me once for real. Now you know what's like to be really fucked." He scooped up the two duffels of money and slapped Luke across the back of his head. "I'll see you around," he laughed as he locked the door behind him.

The clock was ticking now. All Frank could do was worm his way to where Luke was tied, and started to pull at the ankle ropes with his teeth. If they didn't get loose fast enough, they were on the hook for at least two murders, two kidnappings and a heck of a lot of missing money. Frank tried to bite his way through the knots. But this was going to take some serious time. They'd track Malloy down, he thought. What did he say about revenge? The long haul. He and Luke needed to think about the long haul.

ABOUT THE AUTHOR

Tim Brough is the author of the four books, *Black Gloves White Magic*, *Sgt. Vlengles' Revenge*, *First Hand: An Erotic Guide to Fisting*, and *Skin Tight: A Guide to Rubbermen, Macho Fetish and Fantasy*, in addition to *Bounty Hunters and Kick Ass Cops*. He lives on the outskirts of Philadelphia with his partner, Papa Joel. A nominee for Pantheon of Leather's Mister Marcus Hernandez Lifetime Achievement Award, Tim has been a contributor to other's books/websites. His byline has appeared in magazines including *The Leather Journal*, *Frontiers*, *Mach*, and *Powerplay*, in addition to co-publishing/-editing (with Peter Tolos) *Rubber Rebel* and *Vulcan America*, the only American magazines devoted to the rubber fetish.

He's been a Judge for Mr. International Rubber and Mr. East Coast Rubber as well as a four-time moderator of CLAW's annual Erotic Writer's Forum and was featured as the Rubber Buddha on HBO's SEXBYTES, appeared as Brutux Kahn in Zeus/Can-Am production Brutal Kombat and currently serves on the Board of Delta International as club secretary.

www.ingramcontent.com/pod-product-compliance
Lightning Source LLC
Chambersburg PA
CBHW051123260626
47170CB00005B/1631